THE SNOW WOMAN

AND OTHER
YOKAI STORIES
FROM JAPAN

THE SNOW WOMAN
AND OTHER YOKAI STORIES FROM JAPAN

Noboru Wada

Translated by **William Scott Wilson**
Illustrations by **Haruna Wada**

TUTTLE Publishing
Tokyo | Rutland, Vermont | Singapore

Contents

PART 5 WHEN TENGU STILL LIVED AMONG US

PART 6 YAMAMBA MOUNTAIN WITCHES

PART 7 YOKAI AND SHAPE-SHIFTERS, ONE AFTER ANOTHER

PART 12 BAFFLING STORIES OF REMARKABLE PEOPLE

PART 13 STORIES FROM THE SAMURAI ERA

PART 14 HAIR-RAISING STORIES FROM THE NOT-SO-DISTANT PAST

A Ghostly Walk through the Old Province of Shinshu

The Setting

The ghost stories and strange tales that make up this book are set in the ancient Japanese province of Shinshu, or Shinano (now Nagano Prefecture), located in the center of Japan's main island of Honshu, a region intersected by three mountain ranges, mist-covered streams and a number of large and fast-flowing rivers. Over 80 percent of the area is covered with forests of larch, cedar, cypress and red pine. Shinshu has long been considered a dark and cold place, but isolated villages have been scattered here and there since perhaps the eleventh century, and some of the primitive paths used originally by the early hunters and gatherers were eventually developed into roads to accommodate trade in linen, horses, animal hides and *azusa* wood, prized for making bows. Yet, even these roads were considered hazardous and remote as they traversed high passes and deep ravines, and this further accounted for Shinshu's comparative isolation from other populated areas of Japan.

The area was not completely out of the realm of the central Japanese government, however, and in the eighth century Shinshu was established as one of the sixty provinces of the country, administered by a district governor chosen from among local powerful clans. Eventually, wealthy farmers took positions as village headmen under the auspices of the nobility, and a loose hierarchy existed even in the most isolated villages and hamlets.

This combination of the isolation, the daily submergence in nature, the homogeneity of the population, as well as the generational strong sense of place would be the fecund matrix for the stories collected here.

The Stories

Traditional stories, whether, supernatural or not, grow best, like trees, in a place where they are nurtured by the area from which they come. Very few influences are introduced to dilute their flavor, and they grow and mature with their roots in the local soil. With a population that is ever moving from place to place, such as our own, local stories are soon forgotten or simply become irrelevant. If, on the other hand, one passes daily by a pond or path connected to some event in the past, that event will likely live on as a tale of some sort and be passed down to the next generation. The travelers walking the roads and paths through Shinshu would no doubt have added their own strange stories to the mix as they sat around the braziers at their inns at night over sake and other fare.

As for a daily submergence in nature, we moderns have next to none of that, as can be witnessed on almost any thoroughfare with our morning and evening commutes to work, work that is mostly done indoors. The wonder and mysteries of what was long ago our natural environment is shut off from us except for perhaps brief camping trips in the summer, to which we ride in our automobiles and set up our tents in designated spots. Traditional stories, on the other hand, often spring from unexplainable encounters with weather events, animals or even insentient things such as rocks or trees that suggest a liminal world in our very midst. We will not have such experiences seated in front of our computers.

The homogeneity of the Japanese people is another factor that suggests common beliefs and cultural experiences that would lead to the acceptance and belief in eerie stories told to neighbors that might otherwise be disregarded as fantasy or outright lies. The underlying belief in the gods and buddhas of even the most modern Japanese, their experiences as a nation, and their everyday social norms contrast notably with the "melting pot" society made up of various languages, beliefs and cultures that is common in other countries, such as the US. Without a strong shared sense of place, identity and memory, traditional stories such as the ones collected in this book can sometimes be lost.

A word should be added concerning the previously mentioned gods and buddhas in this regard.

A fundamental tenet of the ancient native Shinto religion is that the natural world is permeated with a sort of divine energy that is manifested in everything from huge boulders and trees to invisible entities that can help or hinder us according to the reverence we pay them. There is a huge pantheon of the latter to which prayers are delivered for everything from safe childbirth to good harvests to traffic safety to success in exams. Large shrines to these gods which are visited daily are erected in urban areas, while small ones are found in deep forests or even along a roadside. All indicate an invisible presence of some sort, and all are greeted with a reverential clap of the hands.

Buddhism, although not introduced to the Japanese until the mid-first millennium CE, is also ubiquitous throughout the archipelago, and is rich with a population of major and minor gods, buddhas, saints and demons. Such supernatural beings—like the gods of Shinto—can be associated with certain holy locales or can be appealed to anywhere.

What is pertinent to the ghost stories encountered here is a traditional belief in a liminal world that often makes itself known through otherwise inexplicable events.

Delivery

It is important to note that traditional stories like the ones in this book were not written down until modern times, and were originally passed from generation to generation through the spoken word. Again, whether from the proprietor of an inn entertaining tired guests, or from grandparents to their children and grandchildren on cold winter nights as they sat together warming themselves in their isolated farmhouse, they were no doubt told with drama and with an incantatory flare. Wada Noboru, the collector and re-teller of these stories, has noted in his introduction to the original Japanese books in which his versions of these stories were published, that it is necessary to preserve such a style in order to portray, not just their structural content, but their psychological and emotive content as well, and in writing them down, he assumes that Japanese readers will have a certain cultural understanding of nuance and conversational drift—which Western readers might find difficult to follow. Thus, in translation, we have felt it necessary to rework a sentence here, or a paragraph there, in order to prevent any confusion as to what exactly is happening, while not diluting the emotional impact that would have been felt by the native listeners of these tales. And we trust that the hair will rise on the necks of our modern readers just as it did on those eager children and tired travelers a hundred years ago.

The Characters

The collection of tales presented here, then, is a sort of story map of the old province of Shinshu, and we are accompanied on our journey by various yokai, ghosts, apparitions or the recollections of just strange people who have a found a place of permanent residence there. As many of these characters may not be familiar to the Western reader, we present here a short list of definitions of who and what we are to encounter.

- ♠ *Amanojaku* (天邪鬼): Literally, a heavenly evil demon. Perverse demons, sometimes seen as being trampled by Buddhist temple guardian gods.

- ♠ *Azukitogi* (小豆研ぎ): A strange noise sounding like azuki beans being washed or ground. The noise is usually the work of a yokai.

- *Daija* (大蛇): A huge serpent. Large snakes, usually black, were often considered the *nushi*, or guardian, of a pond or river. They could turn into dragons, or even humans, and were immensely strong forces, either neutral, good or evil.

- *Hitotsume Kozo* (一つ目小僧): A small yokai with one eye in the middle of its forehead, usually dressed as a Buddhist acolyte.

- *Kappa* (河童): Literally, "river child." A small water sprite that likes to entice people or animals into rivers or lakes where they drown. They can sometimes be appeased by offerings of cucumbers or rice cakes. A dish of water on their heads give them their strength, without which they are helpless and can be subdued.

- *Kitsune* (狐): A fox that is a yokai, often regarded as a troublemaker and shape-shifter that will lead people astray. It can, however, possess benevolent traits. It is thought of as the messenger of Inari, the god of harvest, and sometimes confused with the god itself.

- *Ko-oni* (小鬼): Literally "child demon," more like an imp.

- *Obake* (お化け): The kanji character simply means "change" and so a literal translation of this word would be "shape-shifter."

- *Onbu-obake* (負んぶお化け): A yokai that likes to be carried piggyback.

- *Oni* (鬼): A demon, sometimes associated with messengers from Hell.

- *Onibaba* (鬼婆): A witch or hag; sometimes an evil old lady living in the mountains who often traps and eats people, especially children.

◊　*Onyudo* (お入道): Can mean either a lay Buddhist priest, or a large monster or demon. It is sometimes visualized as a huge serpent.

◊　*Tanuki* (狸): A type of yokai that looks similar to a raccoon dog, but is accredited with being able to change shape into human form. They enjoy bewitching people and leading them astray.

◊　*Tengu* (天狗): The kanji characters mean "heavenly dogs," but Tengu demons were first seen as raptors with human heads who caused injuries or calamities. They later evolved into human form, able to fly, sometimes with wings, at other times with the aid of fans. Some Tengu have red faces and long noses. Most are mischievous, but others are protectors of Buddhism. They are considered excellent swordsmen and some have esoteric knowledge of medicine.

◊　*Yamamba* (山姥): A mountain witch. Literally, an old lady who lives in the mountains.

◊　*Yokai* (妖怪): Usually defined as ghosts, apparitions or goblins, the two kanji characters that make up this word simply mean spooky or mysterious. The first kanji can even mean "attractive" or "interesting." Yokai can appear in almost every form imaginable, from a one-legged umbrella to women with necks longer than snakes, to little girls who haunt the showers at elementary schools.

◊　*Yuki-onna* (雪女): An ephemeral female snow ghost. Usually appears during snow storms, and sometimes foreshadows the death of the person who sees it.

◊　*Yukinko* (雪ン子): A child snow demon. Often playful, but can also bring ill luck to a person who sees one.

◊ *Yurei* (幽霊): A ghost, spirit or apparition. The character 幽 indicates something hazy, indistinct or dim; while 霊 means soul or spirit.

Religious figures and terms

◊ *Enma* (閻魔): The king of Hell. He holds a scroll listing all of one's bad deeds.

◊ *Hachiman* (八幡): God of archery and war in both the Shinto and Buddhist religions. He is considered to be able to predict when a person will die, and by extension is also known as a god of determining one's fate.

◊ *Inari* (稲荷): Literally, the carrier of grain, he/she is the god of harvest and fecundity. Inari is often confused with a fox god, statues of which adorn the god's shrine, but the fox is actually the god's messenger.

◊ *Jizo* (地蔵): One of the many bodhisattvas, those who vow to attain enlightenment and to save suffering beings. Jizo (literally, "Earth Repository") is one of the most popular bodhisattvas in Japan, his statues placed in temples, on the roadside, anywhere people might pass. He is known especially as the savior of the souls of dead children, of travelers and of small animals He typically appears as a small shaven-headed child, adorned with a red bib.

◊ *Namu Amida Butsu* (南無阿弥陀仏): This can be translated as "Hail to the Buddha Amida." As a mantra, it is considered to have beneficial power.

◊ *Nembutsu* (念仏): A chant or mantra repeated over and over by Pure Land Buddhists and Buddhists of other sects.

◊ *The Pure Land* (浄土): The Western Pure Land of Amida Buddha (a transcendental, not historical, Buddha.) It is a paradise that is a sort of halfway house to Nirvana. Members of the Pure Land sects pray to be reborn there.

⚑   *Yamabushi* (山伏): Literally, "those who lie down in the mountains," the term refers to a practitioner of the esoteric Buddhist sect of Shugendo. The monks lived in the mountains, practicing austerities in order to gain spiritual powers. They usually traveled alone, wandering from place to place. Their acquired powers were sometimes used simply for their own whims.

Yesterday and Today

As noted above, in times past, odd occurrences and things that went bump in the night were explained by the premodern Japanese in accordance with their religious beliefs and their imaginations. Concepts of the myriad gods—both benevolent and malicious—and the different levels of existence a person passed through in Buddhist theology were just a stone's throw from believing in goblins, ghosts and reincarnated souls. Modern science and technology, of course, would banish such beliefs to the dustbins of history.

But apparently not. The final stories in this book, which are set in relatively recent times, would hint that there is still a thirst for the unexplained and the macabre, and the author has suggested that such stories, even if only supported by rumor and gossip, may become the ghost stories of the future, and so has included them in this collection.

During this translator's time in Japan, he experienced many instances when friends, both young and old, would offer supernatural explanations for events they found inexplicable by science. Perhaps the occasion most personal to me was an episode that took place in the 1970s, when I was living in a small apartment in the countryside, an hour from the big city of Nagoya. My rooms looked out into a narrow ravine through which tumbled a clear stream bordered by Japanese cypress and other evergreens.

A very peaceful and secure setting, I thought. But one morning as I was about to leave to teach my English classes, I found that my kitchen—the only way in and out of the apartment—was occupied by a very large black snake and I felt that being late for work was probably the better part of valor. Eventually, the snake moved on, and so did I. When I spoke to my landlady about this however, she was both surprised and pleased, informing me that the snake was likely the *nushi,* or protector, of the area, and that it was checking me out to its satisfaction. This she said in all seriousness, without a hint of just trying to placate me. When I mentioned this to one of my older students, expecting at least a wry smile, he did not bat an eye. After a while, neither did I.

Never dismiss anything out of hand.

Acknowledgments

I would like to thank Noboru Wada for allowing me the privilege of translating the stories he has collected and re-told in this book so that they can be shared with a worldwide audience, and Haruna Wada for her beautiful illustrations. I would also like to extend a special thanks to my friends and colleagues who have encouraged me in my endeavors of translation throughout the years: Kate Barnes, Gary Haskins, Jim Brems, John Siscoe, Jack Whisler, Tom Levidiotis, Dr. Daniel Medvedov, Dr. Justin Newman and Roshi Bill Durham. As always, my deepest bow of gratitude to my mentor, the late Ichikawa Takashi (who told me a number of stories similar to those in this book), and to my late professors of Japanese and classical Chinese, Drs. Richard McKinnon and Hiraga Nobuo.

Finally, a sweeping hats off to my extraordinary editor at Tuttle Publishing, Ms. Cathy Layne.

—William Scott Wilson

PART 1

TALES OF THE SNOW WOMAN

The Legend of the Snow Woman

A long time ago, in a village at the foot of Mount Shirouma, there lived two hunters, father and son, Mosaku and Minokichi. They were both quite skillful hunters and walked about this mountain and that, hunting bears and mountain goats, returning home every day.

However, something happened one winter. For some reason, they had not caught even a rabbit the entire day.

"This is the first time for such a thing!"

"What a strange day, huh."

Mumbling such things, they talked together as they walked on. Meanwhile, a heavy snow began to fall, and eventually they felt that they could hardly continue on. It was still daytime, but it grew dark, and they were no longer sure of their direction.

Looking up at the sky, Mosaku paused and exclaimed that this was certainly strange and out of the ordinary, and advised Minokichi that under such conditions they were going to become lost and would not be able to go back down to the village. For now, he said, they should look for a cave and prepare to wait it out.

The two of them quit hunting and walked around looking for a cave, but could find nothing. The snow was such that they could hardly keep their eyes open, turning into a blizzard like one they had never experienced.

Father and son continued to walk around lost, now to the east, now to the west, until their minds became dim, feeling that the mountain they should have known well was now like a foreign land. Blindly, the two of them silently descended a slope, and of a sudden came upon what appeared to be a mountain hut there in the snow.

"Ah, we're saved!"

"Looks like we can spend the night here!"

The two went inside and quickly began to feel better.

"Well now, Minokichi, let's light a fire so we can warm up fast," Mosaku said, encouraging his son who appeared to be falling asleep.

At last, the two of them sat next to a fire they had lit in the hearth, and while drying their clothes, hungrily ate some dried jerky, somehow returning to their usual spirits. Nevertheless, with the day's fatigue, the two of them quickly fell into a deep sleep. Outside, the snow was falling peacefully in drifts, just as before, and the night deepened, falling into profound darkness.

Then suddenly Minokichi heard a voice calling him: "Excuse me ... Master Minokichi ..."

"What is this?" Minokichi rubbed his ears, wondering how it was possible for a person to be calling on a night like this, so deep in the mountains. But then, sure enough, someone was calling his name.

Getting up, he looked in the direction of the door, and right there stood a beautiful woman dressed in a pure white kimono, her hair glistening and wet. Astonished, Minokichi asked who she was, and she silently moved to his side.

"Master Minokichi, at last I have been able to come to you. I have watched you from afar, driven by feelings of love as you have gone from mountain to mountain."

"What ... what are you saying?" Minokichi exclaimed, but a strange feeling was moving deep inside of him. He wanted to embrace her, but checked himself, and the woman said, "For tonight, we can go only this far, for I am returning home now. But if you want me, you cannot tell anyone we met like this tonight. No matter what, you must not speak of this!"

"Yes, yes! For sure," he answered quickly, not wanting to let the woman go. "But you ... who ... ?" Yet, as he was about to ask, the woman moved to the door. He called out for her to wait, but as he did, she had already disappeared, and only a flurry of snow circled through a chink in the door.

Wondering what this could be, Minokichi returned to

himself and looked over toward his father, who, to Minokichi's sudden shock, seemed to be spitting blood.

"Father! Father! What's the matter?" he wailed. But no
matter how many times he shook him, his father's eyes would
not open and gradually he stopped breathing. Minokichi
cried throughout the night and waited for the dawn.

While the visit of the woman that night haunted him,
Minokichi shouldered the body of his father, returned to the
village and buried Mokichi with deep respect.

◊   ◊   ◊

Two and then three years passed. Minokichi's skill in hunting
increased day by day, his reputation in the village grew, and
there was talk that he would surely fetch a good bride. And
soon it happened.

One night during a blizzard, Minokichi was fashioning
straw ropes, when there was someone knocking on the door.
Wondering who it could be on a night like this, and thinking it strange, he stood up, opened the door, and there was a
pretty woman he had never seen before.

"I apologize for bothering you on a night like this," she
said, "but I am on a journey, and have become more and more
lost. I finally saw this light, and made my way here. Could you
not let me stay over for just one night?"

Hearing this, the kindhearted Minokichi replied, "Well,
there's really nothing here to entertain you with, and it's not
much of a place to stay," but had her come inside. "I don't
know where you're from, but please come close to the hearth
and warm yourself up."

"Thank you so much," she quietly replied.

Minokichi offered her a fur pelt cushion and made her
some rice gruel. Exclaiming that the gruel looked delicious
and apologizing for being such a bother, she smiled and accepted his offer. Minokichi felt that her bearing was wonder-
fully charming and sweet and was completely taken by her.

Outside, the blizzard showed no signs of abating.

"Well now, it looks as though you may not be able to continue your journey tomorrow," Minokichi said. "Why don't you stay here, recover your strength and then continue on?"

As the blizzard did not show signs of letting up even the next day, the woman was detained again, and said that she would trouble Minokichi for a little while longer. And so it seemed that she was resolved.

A number of days passed, their relationship developed into one of trust and confidence, and the woman, little by little, talked about herself. Her name was Koyuki, which means "little snow," both of her parents had passed away, and she was on her way to the home of some acquaintance who lived far away.

Minokichi began to grow more and more attached to Koyuki, and when she made ready to go, he stopped her, saying, "What do you think? Shouldn't we live here together at my house? Even if you were to go to that other place, you wouldn't be treated as well, I think." With such kind words, she nodded assent, and at some point started cooking up a delicious rice meal, offering it to Minokichi. In the end, they became husband and wife.

The two of them then passed many happy days, children were born, and after ten years, yet a fifth child was growing up. The village people declared that Minokichi must be very happy, and looked at him with envy.

Then one day there was a heavy snowstorm, and Minokichi's family had gathered around the hearth. After a while, the children went off to their beds by ones and twos, leaving the husband and wife alone. The blizzard outside shook the door, interrupting their conversation. Minokichi then remembered the strange event on the mountain when he was young, that took place on a night just like this.

Minokichi searched for the memory that was deep in his breast, and he started to talk about the night his father died. "Because it's you, I can talk about this strange experience . . . now that I think of it, the woman who came to the door that night must have been a Yuki-onna snow woman."

Suddenly Koyuki yelled out, "You!" and glared at Minokichi with a terrifying face. "Ahh, now it's finished!" she shouted, and her eyes were flooded with tears. "This is so sad. I told you not to talk about that night and believed you wouldn't, but you've broken your promise!"

"What?" Minokichi cried. "That was you, then?"

"This is the end!" Koyuki screamed. "In fact, I was just now about to take your life, but can't because of our darling children! Ahhh!" As Koyuki burst out crying, she ran outside.

"Koyuki! Koyuki!" Drowning in tears, Minokichi leapt out into the blizzard, but she had already disappeared. The only movement was the silent falling of the snow.

In the coming day, the snow stopped falling, and Minokichi was able to climb up the mountain; but though he looked and looked for Koyuki, he could not see her.

Thereafter, he continued to look out at Mount Shirouma, and would call her name over and over.

"Koyuki! Koyuki!"

Minokichi could be seen like this every day, but his was the fate of a man who had broken his promise. He never saw Koyuki again.

The Sweet-Tempered Snow Woman

At the mention of a Yuki-onna snow woman, the usual reaction is one of dread, but there are also gentle and sweet-tempered Yuki-onna in this world.

One day, an old man told his wife, "Well, I'll be going now," and, shouldering a pack his wife had prepared, headed off toward the mountains. The old man was a charcoal maker and his job required long journeys into the mountains to collect the wood he would use to burn for charcoal. So in the pack were, of course, provisions for food, but also medicines for ailments such as colds and hip and foot pain—all prepared for him by his wife.

The old man assured his wife that, with this, he wouldn't get sick at all, but checked each medicine that she had been careful to include. His wife responded that she would be praying that he would bring them back unused. The old man replied, "Even then, if I don't get sick myself, I may give them to others." He then climbed up the mountain slope through the snow that had just started to fall and went deeper and deeper into the interior.

"I'm almost at that lone cedar tree—that will be a good place to shelter," he mumbled as the snow fell more heavily, soon becoming a blizzard and finally coming up to his thighs. Each time he took a step, the snowshoes he was wearing sank into the snow. Moreover, he felt that the hut where he stayed while he was working was far off, and that he could no longer move on.

He felt that if he could get as far as that lone cedar, there would be, as always, a sort of snow cave beneath it where he would be able to take a rest. And so, he pushed himself on.

"Ah, there it is at last," the old man exclaimed, spotting the huge tree standing in the dusk. The tree shook back and forth in the cold wind, and at its base, the snow drift had piled up more than usual, almost covering over the cave, so when he finally reached it, he wondered if it would be better to try and make it to the hut. Becoming uneasy, he looked again at the snow cave beneath the tree, and there in the dark of the cave, something seemed to be moving, perhaps a fox or a wolf. Just then, a beautiful woman with long hair, dressed in a white kimono came out from within and looked steadily at the old man with a sad expression.

Somehow, she had perhaps seen that he was going to sleep under the cedar tree, and had felt sorry for him. She must have thought that the old man had been caught in the snow storm on his journey and needed to rest.

"Are you all right?" the old man asked. "What are you doing here?"

"I was trying to make it home through the blizzard, but then my stomach began to hurt," she said, and her eyes filled with tears.

"That's terrible," the old man exclaimed, and told her that he was carrying some medicine for stomach troubles. He put down his pack in front of the cave, rummaged through it, took out the medicine for stomach ailments, and handed it to the woman together with his gourd full of water.

Thanking the old man, she drank it down in a gulp.

"I'll be better now for sure," she said, and with that lay down on her side.

When the old man saw this, he thought that she might freeze to death, and said, "Wait, I'll light a fire for you," and, bringing some firewood into the snow cave, began to prepare a fire. "Well then, while you warm yourself up, I'll go on outside." But as he said this, and turned to look in her direction, the figure of the woman had disappeared.

"What?" The old man ran outside in confusion, but there were not even footprints in the snow. "I wonder if she was a Yuki-onna?" he thought. "If she was, she was quite tender-hearted," and once again shouldered his pack. The snow had become even heavier, but he finally reached his hut.

After this, he put all his efforts into his charcoal-burning work every day. It was a lonely job, but he was able to make the charcoal that people praised him for, and he worked happily away.

◊   ◊   ◊

After many days had passed, a blizzard once again blew through the mountain. On such a night, there was nothing for it but to go quickly to sleep, so the old man grilled just a bit of rice cake, ate it and soon crawled under his futon.

This night, the door rattled back and forth, and he felt uneasy in the darkness. Unable to sleep he started thinking about the day he had climbed the mountain and encountered the strange woman. "If that was a Yuki-onna," he thought, "I would have been cursed and died. But I'm still alive, so maybe she was just a traveler."

Certainly, there were many stories from long ago about village people who had encountered snow women and had died. So, even supposing that she was really a Yuki-onna, as he had given her some medicine, perhaps she had looked the other way and thought of him as different.

Just as he was thinking this, it seemed as though there was a knocking on the door.

"There have been many blizzards before, but none like this, and there is little reason for people to be coming here now," the old man thought, pulling his futon over his head and staying quite still. But, yes, it seemed that someone was there, so he pulled himself together and stood up. Resigning himself, he asked, "Yes . . . who is it?" and opened the door.

With a rush, the snow blew in, and the old man stood momentarily in surprise. There at his feet, some things had been thrown down and scattered about. When he picked one up, he saw that it was a special kind of mochi rice cake, called sasamochi, wrapped in bamboo leaves.

"Huh?" And there were four of them.

The old man hurried outside and looked around, but there

were no footprints in the snow, just as there had been none under the cedar tree some time ago.

"This, for sure, is from the Yuki-onna," he thought. "A Yuki-onna with a sense of gratitude." He now remembered the Yuki-onna's tear-filled eyes, and thought that people should stop judging others to be good or bad according to their own favorable circumstances.

Thinking such things, he opened one of the bamboo leaves, and there on the leaf were the Chinese characters for "thank you," written in charcoal.

The old man finished up his work, returned to his village, and told his wife that a good thing had happened, praising the Yuki-onna.

But the villagers believed that he had been bewitched by a Kitsune fox demon or something like that, and did not take him seriously; and the old man regretted many times that he had burned up those bamboo leaves in the hut's hearth.

The Snow Child's Red Straw Sandal

It is said that, a long time ago, when the people of the village of Hakuba went toward the mountains, they often saw the figures of beautiful Yukinko snow children. The Yukinko—older and younger sisters—were always together, were dressed in thin robes, and played gracefully in the glittering snow-covered fields at dusk.

Well then, there was in this village a man named Usaka who was well-known as a bear hunter. In winter, when bears were hibernating, he would stay in his mountain hut and make charcoal. As he made the charcoal, however, he thought incessantly about his granddaughter, wondering if she was recovering from an illness that kept her in bed sleeping and unable to stand up. Someone had told him that she would quickly be cured if she put on the straw sandals of a Yukinko. Usaka thought constantly about this as he made his charcoal.

One evening, when he was asleep in his hut, he was awoken by the clear sound of a bell from somewhere outside. Peeking stealthily through a chink in the door, he was taken aback in surprise. Two otherworldly little girls with long silver hair were playing affectionately right before his eyes. From time to time, they would laugh together in beautiful warbling voices. Just as he was taken by this sight and wondering who they were, his eyes were caught by the red-colored straw sandals the sisters were wearing.

"Ah, could these be the sandals?" Usaka thought as his mind went quickly to his granddaughter. But he considered the warnings of the villagers who said that Yukinko are fearful spirits who confuse people in the snowy mountains, and take their souls, so one should be careful. There are stories of those who, captivated by their alluring beauty, have never returned home again.

Nevertheless, he started to think that even if they were such evil spirits, just taking their sandals would not be so bad.

In this way, Usaka began to consider just when he might go out to take the sandals, and watched intently for an opportunity. But in the end the girls were so cute that he had no desire to steal from them, so he gave up his plan and decided to go back to his charcoal-making for a while. Just at that moment, the Yukinko left the place near the hut and went off toward the top of the mountain. But then he looked again...

"What's this?" Was it not a single red straw sandal falling from the sky onto the snow? "I've got one," he exclaimed. Usaka ran over, picked up the sandal and put it into his breast pocket. "Ahh," he thought, "with this I'll be able to cure my granddaughter's illness."

With this thought, Usaka returned to his hut, rubbed his eyes and envisaged his granddaughter getting out of bed and being able to stand. Yet, just then, he was struck by a guilty conscience, for surely, if it were a Yukinko who had lost her sandal, she would feel very sad. Thinking this way and that, he did not know what to do.

Finally, with the straw sandal still in his breast pocket, he started up the slope, with the snow still falling. Making his way through snowdrift after snowdrift, he looked for the snow children and finally stood before the mountain peak. But as he had been walking through the deep snow, a blizzard had enveloped the mountain, and his consciousness grew dim. Finally, he collapsed into the snow.

Just then, music echoed from somewhere uncertain, and he felt that he might be in Heaven.

After that, a long time elapsed.

When Usaka awoke from his dream, the blinding light of morning flashed before his eyes. And at the same time, the Yukinko sisters were laughing and peering at his face. The elder sister showed him a red straw sandal and said something. Simultaneously, the younger sister pulled a tiny red straw sandal from her own breast pocket, and held it in front of him.

"Please give this to her, old man," she said. It was not the sandal at all, because she was clearly wearing her own. Usaka was taken aback. "With this," she continued, "the child will surely recover from her illness."

Filled with confusion, Usaka was unable to respond, and while in this state, was aware that the Yukinko had suddenly disappeared.

Now all that remained was the red straw sandal he was holding in his hand that had been given to him by the younger sister, and thanks to that sandal, his granddaughter became well and went running about. After that, Usaka thought every day that if the Yukinko appeared again, he would introduce them to his granddaughter and let them play together.

The Snow Child That Fell from the Sky

When people talk about Yukinko snow children, it seems a matter of fact that they are talking about girls. But this is a story about a Yukinko who was a boy.

In a village at the foot of Mount Hakuba, there was a cute little girl by the name of O-mitsu. Near the end of the year—the twenty-eighth day of December—everyone in O-mitsu's household started making mochi rice cakes in preparation for the New Year. But as O-mitsu was only six years old, she did not help, but instead, innocently played with a ball on the veranda.

That day, the sky grew cloudy and after a while, snow and hail started to fall.

"Yaa! It's really coming down," O-mitsu shouted, looking up at the sky. Just then, a big lump of hail fell, kerplop, and rolled right in front of her. And as she looked, a cute, white-skinned little boy came out from the middle of that lump of hail. Then he raised his hands as a sort of "Hey!"

O-mitsu looked surprised, but the little boy said, "Will you let me play ball, too?" in a limpid voice. When she let him play, as he had asked, it was clear that he was more skillful with the ball than O-mitsu.

Just then, her grandmother came out bringing a platter piled high with the just-finished mochi. "Now then, where did this child come from?" she asked, cocking her head. "I've never seen such a cute little child as this."

As the old lady gazed at him, the boy said, "From there," pointed at the sky, and said nothing more.

O-mitsu then said, "He came down with the hail," and her grandmother and other household members gathered near.

"This must be one of the Yukinko we've heard about," they said, all delighted at their good luck. "If that's so, then the god of the New Year must have delivered him to us."

And so the little boy started living with O-mitsu's family.

This story spread around the village, and the headman declared, "This is a sign that this year will be a prosperous one," and sent out an official notice that every household should be decorated with special large branches of pines and bamboo.

In O-mitsu's family, it was even said that in the future, when O-mitsu grew up, it would be good to make the little boy a son-in-law. O-mitsu was also very pleased, and played happily with the boy on New Year's Day.

◊　◊　◊

The fourth day of the New Year was Sankuro-no-Hi—a festival praying for the absence of illness and disasters. In a broad open space, the villagers erected a large pillar, stacked against it all the decorative pine branches from each house, and lit them on fire.

Everyone said, "Well, the fire is burning quite brightly, so it must be because the snow child came to us. It will be a prosperous year for sure," and called over O-mitsu and the Yukinko. But although they called for him to come, the little boy stood stock still and would not move. Not understanding what this might mean, the man in charge of lighting the fire said, "I'll show this to the Yukinko," and lit some straw which ignited into flames.

"Oh my, oh my," O-mitsu exclaimed and, taking the snow boy's hand, walked toward the burning straw. Suddenly she felt the boy's hand loosen from hers as the flames moved toward him and started to swallow him up. He seemed to rise up with the fire and disappear into the sky.

"Wait! Don't go away!" O-mitsu cried in vain. But that was the last time they ever saw the boy.

As soon as the fire went out, a heavy snow began to fall, and though that year was a prosperous one, people often said with regret that if the boy had stayed another while, it would have been more prosperous yet.

For her part, O-mitsu was unable to forget the days spent with the Yukinko, and even as an old lady, told the story to her grandchildren over and over.

PART 2

WHY ARE DRAGONS' EYES SO SAD?

The Lute-Playing Priest
Who Saved a Village

A long time ago there was a lute-playing priest traveling through northern Shinano Province. The priest was nearly blind, but was very good at playing the lute, and the beautiful quality of sound emanating from it soothed the hearts of people tired from their work.

Well then, one autumn day, the priest was crossing a mountain on his way from a village when, as he was groping and pushing his way through the leaves of the bamboo grass, he came out onto the bank of a large pond. He could not see it very well but could recognize what it was. Around it, the brightly colored autumn leaves had grown thick, and it seemed to be a good place to take a rest.

"Ah, how good this feels," the priest exclaimed as he wiped off his sweat, scooped up the clean water in his hands and drank. Feeling much better and thinking that he might polish his talent, took up the lute to play. At length, its pleasant sound moved across the surface of the pond and echoed across to the other side.

Then, to his surprise, waves arose across the surface of the pond, and from its center, a deep voice emerged. "Oh, what an excellent tune! Wouldn't you please play another? And since you'll be playing it as a favor, I'll restore your eyesight for you."

Just as he was asked, the priest played another tune, and when he had finished his eyes that could not see until then suddenly became clear and were filled with a dazzling light. At the same time, a dragon rose from the middle of the pond and said, "How do you feel? You can see me well, I guess."

"Thank you so much," the priest responded. "Is there no

way I can show my gratitude to you for restoring my sight?"

"No, no," the dragon replied. "Your music was quite thanks enough. But in return, please play another tune, the saddest one you know." And as soon as this was asked, the priest responded to the dragon's request. The priest then said that he would be off and stood up to go.

"Wait just a little," the dragon interjected, detaining him for a moment. "There is something I would like to confess, but only to a kind-hearted person like you."

Thinking this a bit unusual, the priest stared at the dragon's face.

"All right," the dragon continued. "You must never repeat what I am telling you. If, in the end, you should reveal this to anyone, your life will end." With this warning, he went on. "What I am going to tell you is this. Lately, the people of the village you have just left do not know the true value of water. Thus, they use it wastefully, argue among themselves over it, and this leads me to despair. I cannot watch this in silence."

The priest listened quietly as the dragon spoke.

"I have made up my mind. On the night of the sixteenth of this month, I am going to break down the dams of this pond and assail the village with its floodwaters. So it would be good if you left this area and evacuated to somewhere safe. Well, I think you understand."

With these words, the dragon disappeared into the middle of the pond. The priest gave a great sigh, his eyes filling with tears, and suppressed the hammering of his heart in his chest. The gentle faces of the people in the village that he had just passed through, their simple stories and their innocently playing children floated before him.

"Ahh, ahh!" the priest lamented as he stood up to go, wondering what to do, and unable to decide. He knew that if he told the dragon's secret to the villagers and saved them, that he himself would die. Crawling into a cave there in the mountain, his head in his hands, he passed several days without being able to move.

Yet, hour by hour, the night of the sixteenth drew near. Just

then, the priest recalled the teaching of the Buddha, and felt
that he had been quite lacking in faith. Aware that without
that faith, human life had no value, he stood up to go, his eyes
now full of a light that had not been there. Helping the village
people would come first!

In the instant of being thus resolved, the priest ran down
the mountain, yelling to the villagers, telling everyone the secret. Yet few people believed him, and there were even some
who cocked their heads and wondered out loud if he had
gone crazy.

But the priest insisted it was true and that they must believe him. Climbing up the village fire watchtower, he clanged
the bell over and over, until some of the people thought that
the priest must be telling the truth. Gathering up their household possessions, more and more of them fled to a higher
place on the mountain.

At last, when all of them had left the village, the evening
of the sixteenth finally arrived. The sky suddenly darkened,
there was a thundering sound as the earth shuddered up and
down, and flood waters invaded the village in a single rush.
The people who had fled up the mountain with the priest
watched as their homes were washed away, along with their
rice paddies and vegetable fields. Still, though they raised
their crying voices, they had not lost their lives and, sighing
with relief, said to one another that they were still among the
living, thanks to the priest.

Yet, what had happened to that priest?

The villagers soon began to feel uneasy and, looking
around, found him sitting beneath a pine tree at a slight distance, lamenting with all his heart.

Then, someone pointed to the sky. "What . . . what is that?"
As a black cloud approached, the mountain where the people
had gathered seemed to groan, and the people could see the
eye of a dragon in the midst of the cloud.

The cloud then swirled around the sky and flew far into
the distance. As the people gasped, they noticed that the
priest had disappeared. Thinking that he had been carried

off, they ran in the direction of the fleeing cloud, eventually coming to the pond. But the priest was nowhere to be seen, and there was only a lute, floating back and forth in the ripples on the surface of the pond. The villagers stood on the bank of the pond, lamenting and declaring that the priest had saved them. Sometime later, they began to call the pond Biwa-ike, meaning "Lute Pond" out of gratitude to the priest.

Or so the story goes.

Princess Kurohime and the Black Dragon

This is something that happened several hundred years ago. In the town of Nakano in northern Shinano, lived a beautiful young girl called Princess Kurohime. She was the daughter of Takanashi Masamori, governor of Settsu and lord of Odate Castle, and she was brought up with great affection.

Masamori enjoyed spending time with his daughter, going on walks with her through the mountains and inviting her along for flower-viewing parties.

One spring, Masamori was exchanging sake cups with everyone beneath the cherry blossoms in Higashiyama, when out of nowhere a small serpent approached them. When it drew near, it stopped and raised its head in the direction of where the princess was sitting. In a light mood, Masamori said, "Well, is this serpent thinking it would like to receive some sake from the princess? Princess! Please give this thing some sake from your cup." When the princess did so, the serpent drank the sake in an instant and, slithering away, disappeared into the bushes. "How delightful," said Masamori, clapping his hands and laughing, then returning to his sake.

Well, a few days later, a young samurai arrived at the castle. Not only was his personal appearance in excellent order, but his features were quite refined, and his manners were perfect. Masamori, sitting opposite to him, was very impressed and asked, "Well now, what is your business here?"

"I have come here today," the young man replied, "with a request to make Princess Kurohime my bride."

"What?" Masamori exclaimed in surprise. "To make the princess your bride?" He then asked the young samurai's rank, and again was surprised by the answer.

"I will be very frank and honest with you," the young samurai said. "I am a dragon that lives in the Great Swamp Lake on Mount Shiga."

"This must be a joke!" Masamori said.

"No. In truth, this is just an appearance in which I have come. I am a dragon, but I have the same heart as men, and am drawn to beauty."

"Um . . . ," Masamori interjected.

But the young man went on. "The other day when I encountered the princess, I felt that my heart was taken at first glance. So please, I am asking to make the princess my bride. This is my request."

The young samurai bowed his head deeply and, looking up, stared fixedly into Masamori's eyes.

"That was you in the form of a serpent?" the lord stammered. And he did not give his consent, but politely refused.

The young samurai left the castle with seeming regret, but this would not be the end of his quest.

◊   ◊   ◊

The young samurai did not give up, but later continued to appear at the castle, and repeated the same request. Nevertheless, no matter how often he came, Masamori was firm and did not change his mind.

The lord did not have the courage to tell the princess about this, but while he worried alone, unbeknown to him, the young samurai had been secretly appearing to the princess in her room. Although she was shocked at first, as the days went on, her heart was moved, and she gradually began to think that it would be good to be together with this man. The princess's affection for the young samurai grew day by day, and she wondered how she could obtain her father's consent.

But when Masamori found out that the samurai had been visiting his daughter, he did not understand her heart and, no matter what, was not about to hand her over to the dragon's uncanny incarnation of a samurai. "So," he thought, "I will not allow that thing to step one foot inside the castle," and he ordered his samurai to surround the stronghold. Thus, the castle was strictly guarded; and yet somehow, the young samurai was able to sneak in from somewhere, and appeared before Masamori.

"If I cannot have the princess," he declared, "then I will sacrifice my life."

At this, even a warrior like Masamori shook uncontrollably, and fearfully sank into thought. And then he declared, "All right. I have understood. If you can say a thing like this, I will give you the princess. But there is a condition. Tomorrow, I will ride a horse around the castle twenty-one times. If you can run and keep up with me, the princess is yours."

"Certainly," the young samurai replied, his heart on fire.

Well then, the next day Masamori mounted his favorite well-trained horse, and as soon as the samurai appeared he yelled, "All right! Let's go!" and applied the whip to the horse's flank. The horse galloped off like an arrow shot from a bow. The young samurai followed desperately behind. Three times, four times, five times they circled the castle, and by then, the horse, which had run on the outside of the track, was one circuit ahead. But now they encountered a number of swords that had been planted, blade up, as in a queue, surrounding the castle. The young samurai was surprised and cried out, and even though the horse had galloped wide of the swords, Masamori was unable to avoid them, and his body and feet were stained with blood.

During this time, the princess was shut up in her room, where guards had been stationed. But her heart had been taken by the young samurai and moved by feelings of love, she could only pray that he would be safe.

As for the young samurai, he was finally able to complete the twenty-one circles. But waiting for him were the cold words of Masamori.

"Well, so you finished the circles. But here, let's see your own true form. It should be a blood-stained, pure red monster. Such a monster will not fool the princess."

This was no sooner said than the young samurai instantly manifested his true form of a frightening black dragon. And, spitting flames from its mouth, it rose into the sky. At the same time, huge drops of rain began to fall, and thunder began to roar. While Masamori turned pale and fled inside the castle, the black dragon flew off to the north and east, drenching all the rice paddies and vegetable fields around the castle, causing the dikes of Lake Shiga to burst and loosening the flood waters.

Trembling all over at the uproar outside, the princess pushed the guards aside, and ran to Masamori. "Father! Father! Why did you do such a cruel thing? I cannot stand your acting like this!"

"What are you saying?" Masamori replied. "Don't you understand I was protecting you?"

"No, I don't understand at all!"

While they were talking on like this, the flood waters washed away rice paddies, vegetable fields and houses, and rushed into the castle as well. The princess climbed up to the castle tower and, looking up at the sky, took out the secret magic mirror she kept on herself for self-protection.

"Dragon! Black Dragon!" she cried. "It doesn't matter what happens to me. Please believe that I love you. Please! Will you quiet the storm and save the people?"

Perhaps the dragon heard it, as the sky suddenly brightened and it returned. Taking the princess on its back, it once again rose high into the sky. Watching the princess go, Masamori and his retainers raised their voices together, "Ahh, Princess! Ahh ahh, Princess!" But the princess did not look back and disappeared into the sky.

The Black Dragon alighted on a mountain where there was a calm and peaceful lake. The dragon took the princess to the bottom of the lake, and there they lived, day after day, in peace and happiness.

Even today, people call that mountain Kurohime, and remember her and the dragon.

Koga Saburo Turns into a Dragon

Long ago, there were three brothers who lived in the foothills of Mount Tateshina. The eldest was Taro, the next was Jiro and the youngest, Saburo. Each of them had taken a bride, but only the wife of the youngest, Saburo, was very beautiful; and for this reason, the two elder brothers became jealous.

So one day, Taro and Jiro invited Saburo to go out hunting in the mountain, where they came to a large cavern.

"Saburo, do you know how deep this cavern is?" said Taro.

"I don't know either," said Jiro. "Saburo, why don't you climb down into it and see just how deep it is?"

And the good-natured Saburo replied, "Why yes, I'll be happy to do that."

Holding onto a wisteria vine, Saburo descended into the cavern. When the two elder brothers were sure that he was halfway down, they took a woodman's hatchet they had carried with them, cut the vine and fled home.

Back at home, Saburo's wife became uneasy when he did not return, and questioned Taro and Jiro. The two brothers answered indifferently.

"Well, we don't know what happened to him, do we, Jiro?"

"That's right. Perhaps he was attacked by a bear and may be dead."

The young wife was worried and ran to the mountain, calling Saburo's name. But only echoes came back to her, and in the end, Saburo did not return.

♦   ♦   ♦

Well, for his part, Saburo had made a soft landing, and his life was saved, but there was no way that he could climb up to the top of the cavern. As he thought lovingly of his wife, he knew that he had been tricked by his brothers and was full of woe. Then, somehow, there appeared to be a light in the distance, and he crawled steadily along until the cavern opened into a rather large village. Far in the distance, he could see a mountain range.

In this village, beautiful plum flowers were blooming and people were working the rice paddies and vegetable fields. As Saburo drew near, he gradually forgot about the land above the cavern, and even forgot completely about his wife.

When the villagers saw him, they gathered around in curiosity, "Well, well. A fine young man has come to visit," and right away escorted him to the palatial residence of the wealthiest man in the village. Living there was a beautiful young princess, and Saburo fell in love with her at first sight. The princess, too, fell in love with Saburo, and in the end, they became husband and wife.

As time went by, children were born, and Saburo never thought about the world above at all.

◊   ◊   ◊

Nine years passed, then one day Saburo's memory began to return. "Wait! I have a feeling I lived in another world before this. Yes, I'm certain," he mumbled to himself.

One night, two nights passed, and he came to remember with clarity that he was a person who had lived in the world above. And that he had had a beautiful wife whom he had left behind. Tears trickled down his cheeks in sorrow.

The princess saw this and asked, "Why are you so sad?"

Saburo told her the reason honestly, and on hearing this, the princess became sad herself. Saburo now began to feel for his former wife, and was firm about going home, although the princess desperately tried to discourage him.

"Please, send me back to the world above," he said to her.

The princess, who could see his strong determination, said through her tears, "I am sad, but I imagine that your wife in the world above is even sadder," and gave her permission for him to return. And, furthermore, she instructed him what to do to get to the land above.

"Well then, eat some of this mochi rice cake as you go," she said, and gave him some she had prepared that would never run out no matter how much he ate.

Filling his stomach again and again, as he walked through the world below, it became completely dark. And then, just as the princess had warned him would happen, the air split and he came out into the light. Then he heard voices yelling. "Yah! A dragon!" and children were fleeing at the sight of him.

When Saburo looked down at his body, he had indeed turned into a dragon. His head had emerged from a pond, and he would later know that it was the pond at the Shinraku Temple at the foot of Mount Asama.

Though he had turned into a dragon, Saburo still felt love for his former wife. Filled with sorrow, he headed to Mount Tateshina. But no matter how he looked, he could not find her. Shedding tears, Saburo rushed from mountain to mountain, calling his wife's name over and over. When he got to Lake Suwa, he saw a single ray of light coming toward him, gradually getting brighter and brighter. And at that moment, he heard his wife's voice calling his name.

Saburo raised his head and went toward her voice. Immediately black clouds billowed up, and with them, Saburo's body floated upwards, and he then descended into Lake Suwa. There, his former wife had turned into a dragon out of grief and had been awaiting his return.

Meeting again like this, the two lived forever in Lake Suwa, just as they were.

How the Tenryu River Came to Be

This happened a long time ago, when the gods were still creating the mountains and rivers.

Now, up in Heaven there was a lake just right for the dragon children to play in. During the hot summers, they would splash, *basha basha*, in that lake, just like little human children do today. Now among these dragon children, the most mischievous and naughty was the sturdy dragon child called Fang.

"Hey! Let's play in the lake, hurry up! Don't you wish you had a golden fang like me?" he would say to the other dragon children. But not only did he suffer from the sin of pride, he also lacked respect for the lake of Heaven, romping about and deliberately scattering the water down to earth.

"What a troublesome child!" lamented one of the dragon elders known as the Heavenly Dragon. "He does not know the blessings of water at all," and in the end, got angry and sent him tumbling down to earth.

Fang lost consciousness on the way down, but when he came to, found himself at the top of a high, rocky mountain. Today, they call this Mount Tateshina, but nobody knows what it was called so long ago.

Fang forgot that he had been scolded by the Heavenly Dragon, and thought, "Isn't there someplace around here with a nice pond so I can play in the water?" and looked down from the mountain. Then, directly in front of him, there it was! There it was! Fang ran down and took a flying jump—whoosh!—into the pond. How good it felt!

There was nobody there but him, so he romped and splashed, thoroughly enjoying himself, but in two or three days the water began trickling out, and gradually there was very little left. This did not bother him, and he continued to splash about. But on the tenth day, the water was all gone.

"Ahh! What will I do?" Fang cried while looking at the dried-up pond. And there didn't seem to be any sign of rain.

From the beginning, the Heavenly Dragon and the gods had meant to vex Fang a little, and now conferred once again.

The Heavenly Dragon said, "Let's make the drought go on longer; that should teach him," and in this way they disciplined Fang all the more.

Fang was unaware of what was actually happening and looked up to Heaven. "Water! I need water!" he called out, but there was no response from the heavenly dragon.

Seeing that there was nothing else to be done, Fang decided to return to Heaven, climbed to the top of Mount Tateshina, and, stretching himself out, tried to jump. But Heaven was so far up that he couldn't even grasp the clouds that drifted by. Still, he jumped up two times, then three. Each time, he fell with a thud until his stomach began to hurt. Stretching out his claws, Fang was even more determined to make it up to Heaven, and with flaming eyes and great effort, he continued to jump, lacerating the scales on his belly until they bled. And with each thud of his body, a dent eventually formed in the crags.

"Ahh, I want water . . . ahh," he cried.

This continued for a long time, and finally, with his body in pain and his throat completely dry, he lost consciousness.

In the end, when he came to, there was something like the branch of a tree growing right before his eyes, and a beautiful drop of water was glistening on its very top.

"Ahh! Water!" Trembling with joy, Fang stretched out his lips and tried to take a drink. But when he did so, the drop of water slipped down and rolled out of his mouth's reach. When the disheartened Fang settled down and looked carefully, he could see that what had looked like a branch was actually his own beard that had grown over the long months and years. Thus, because it was a drop of water that had collected on his beard, there was no way that he could get it into his mouth. While he had not been aware of it, Fang's body had grown into a huge, splendid dragon, so big that it could have wrapped itself around the crags more than seven times.

Fang was in amazement at this when a voice came from Heaven, "Fang! Have you at last awakened to the preciousness of water?"

It was the voice of the Heavenly Dragon.

"Yes," Fang replied.

"Very well," said the voice. "If that is so, whatever you do, do not spill the drop of water that is on your beard, but set it down in the pond below. If you are able to do that, we will once again welcome you to Heaven."

"Yes, I will do this," Fang replied. "Absolutely."

With great care, Fang descended the mountain, not spilling the drop of water on his beard, and finally arrived at the pond. Then he dropped the water into the charming pond, and in an instant, the pond was filled with clear, clean water. At the same time, moisture was drawn out from his own body and whenever he moved, his dried scales made the sound of rubbing together.

Still feeling sad, Fang heard the voice from Heaven again, saying "That's fine."

Suddenly the skies grew dark, black clouds appeared and rain started, as heavy as a waterfall. "Well now," the voice thundered, "climb back up on this waterfall of rain."

Hearing this, Fang ran up to the top of Mount Tateshina, scratched his way up through the dark for all he was worth, climbed the waterfall of rain and stood before Heaven.

During that time, the water in the pond overflowed, making a large lake. The water then flowed south, creating a river, which would later be called the Tenryu River, or the River of the Heavenly Dragon. And the lake that was created is the very lake that is known as Lake Suwa in Japan today.

The Tale of Koizumi Kotaro

Long ago in the province of Shinano, there was a village called Shiodadaira, known as a place that was least blessed with water. Though there was a river, there was no water to moisten the rice and vegetable fields.

"If the sun keeps shining like this, we'll be very hard pressed," exclaimed the farmers, throwing up their hands.

The villagers went to the temples and shrines and prayed for rain, but as they feared, no rain fell at all.

Well then, there was a temple of no great size on Mount Dokko, which neighbored Shiodadaira; and in this temple lived a young priest. Because he was still young and single, he was always hoping for a wife.

Then, at the onset of one summer, curiously enough, a beautiful woman began to pass by the temple every night.

"Where in the world are you coming from?" the priest asked, but she only smiled gracefully and did not reveal her identity.

With that, the priest thought rather dearly of her, decided not to ask further of her and simply felt pleased when she came to stay the night. But her departure in the mornings troubled the young man.

Time went by, and the priest began to think that this was all very strange. Which is to say, as a woman living in a countrified area like this, she was endowed with an unusual grace and elegance. And finally, he inquired again, "It's a tedious thing to ask, but could you tell me whereabouts you are coming from?"

"Just from upstream of that river," she replied.

"And, the name of the village?" he continued.

With a faint smile, she answered with a downcast look, "If you ask me such things, I will not come again."

The priest gave up, and thereafter stopped asking her

questions, but thinking that she was no ordinary person, he secretly prepared a silken thread and attached it to her kimono with a needle. He planned to use this a device by which he could follow her home.

Finally, the morning arrived when he could trace her path. When the woman returned home, the priest, led by the thread, followed as she continued on her way. The thread twisted past some bamboo grass that had been dampened in the night dew, descended into the marsh at Mount Dokko, led onto the secluded Saddle Pool within the flow of the San River, and went into a cave on the other side. But this, this was not a place where a person could live.

The priest felt a chill, and just as he peeped into the cave a groan came from inside, and a large Daija snake writhed, in the midst of giving birth. The priest was frightened out of his wits. He fled the place, returned home and continuously chanted a sutra with all his concentration. A little while later, someone knocked on his door.

"Yes, who is it?" the priest responded.

"It's me, as usual. Today, you saw my true form, and as I was pierced by a poisonous needle, I must now die. However, the child that was born will remain in this world, and I am asking you to take care of it."

As he heard the woman's retreating footsteps, the priest was aware of his own deep sin, and continued reciting the sutra. However, he told no one of this, and kept it as a secret.

Well, the child of the Daija that was left at the Saddle Pool was a little boy. Now that the woman had disappeared, he cried continuously every day even when he was playing in the river.

One day, rain fell in torrents after a long drought, the river flooded and the boy was swept a distance of two *ri* down to the village of Koizumi.

"Well, well, a child has floated down here."

"Whose child could this be?"

The villagers talked among themselves like this, but had no idea of who the parents might be.

"If that's so, I'll take care of him," said an old lady who lived alone. She called the child Kotaro, made preparations to bring him up and went around with the child on her hip. Feeling that there was no doubt that the child was entrusted to her by the gods, she brought him up with great care. Until he was five years old, he behaved like a spoiled child and played happily with the village children.

As much as he was given to eat, his stomach was soon empty. "Grandma, I'm hungry! I'm hungry!" he would fuss, and when the food on his plate was not enough, he would clamor, "This is too little! Give me some more!"

"I've never seen a child eat this much," said the old lady to herself, thinking this to be strange, but gave him more as she was told.

And speaking of strange, from the time Kotaro came to the village, rain fell in abundance, and Shiodadaira was never lacking for water. Because of this, new rice fields were created in level areas, and along with vegetable gardens, houses increased as well.

◊   ◊   ◊

Ten years passed.

One would think that Kotaro would become a good worker, but he only ate and slept, ate and slept every day, and the old lady was not the only one to be bothered by this. Naturally, things were heard to be said, and in the end, even the old lady could not keep quiet.

"Kotaro! Enough is enough! There is no reason that someone who doesn't work at your age should just stay in the house," she said firmly.

"You're right. I should be working, too, shouldn't I."

So saying, Kotaro suddenly got up, took a sickle and went off to a nearby mountain. In a short while, he returned with a load of firewood on his back. "Grandma," he said. "I've bound up the wood with wisteria vine, so without unfastening it, take it bit by bit and spread it on the fire."

"Ah! I see," said the old lady happily. "You've worked well!"

"Grandma, as I said, please be careful with this, and take the wood out only bit by bit. The reason is that I have gathered up all the firewood in the mountain and have tied up the bundle very tightly."

He repeated this rather strange thing, but the old lady let out a belly laugh as if to say, "What are you talking about?"

The next day, Kotaro went off to the mountain again. The old lady did not believe what Kotaro had said. She loosened the wisteria vine and the bundle of firewood snapped open instantly and spread throughout the house, finally reaching up to the ceiling. The weight of the firewood crushed the old lady, and in the end, she died.

◊   ◊   ◊

After that, Kotaro climbed up a mountain to the west, where he found a large lake. He thereupon mounted on the back of the dragon that lived there, broke down the dikes around the lake, and drained it of water. Down below, the rough land of Shiodadaira and other villages that had suffered in the past from a lack of water turned into green rice fields and vegetable gardens; but if this is true or not is unknown. It is said that the dragon in that lake was the Daija snake that had given birth to Kotaro.

Or such was the story.

PART 3

THERE ARE ALSO
HALF-WITTED DEMONS

The Demons That Were
Stuck in the Eye by Irises

In a certain place, there lived a very greedy man. When he came of the age to take a wife, he often repeated, "For me, I need to find a woman who doesn't eat, but works hard. Otherwise I won't get married."

One day, when the man was walking over a path through the mountain, someone suddenly appeared from a thicket of kerria bushes. The man was surprised, but when he fixed his gaze a bit, it was a woman, in soiled and dirty clothes. She was tall enough that he had to look up, and her hands were rough and scraggly.

"You startled me! What are you doing here in the mountains?" the puzzled man asked.

"Ahh. Well, I'm someone who doesn't eat, but works very hard, and when there's nothing to do, I sleep." The woman laughed readily.

Hearing this, the man was astonished and took a second look at the woman from the top of her head to the tips of her feet. Her hair was disordered, she had a turned-up nose and she was extraordinarily big, and he thought that she would not be suitable for a wife. Except for one thing . . .

"Did you just say that you don't eat?" he asked.

"Ahh, I never feel like eating," she replied calmly.

"Wonderful! That's just what I've been wanting. I've been thinking that I'd like someone like you as a wife. Would you become my wife from now on?" he asked, and the woman happily assented.

Well then, when he accompanied her back to his house, he saw that she did indeed work very hard. She did not eat a grain of rice and went out to the paddies every day before dawn. When she returned to the house at the end of the day, she did not eat anything.

"You really don't eat at all?" This was just what the man had wanted in a wife, and he couldn't help feeling happy deep inside. But he was also concerned that she never ate a bit of food. And thinking that this was too strange, he asked, "How in the world can this be?"

"Ahh," she said, "I don't eat anything at all, it's true. Instead, I have you eat my portion, and have you grow fat." So even when the man felt full, she would encourage him to eat more and more. And if they ran out of rice, she would return to the house with a bagful on her shoulder.

Looking at the man, you could see that his body was growing plump and his face shone with a glossy light. When his wife looked at him, she said, "Just a little more," and smiled knowingly.

At his wife's words, the man could not help but wonder what she was up to. So one day, he kept a steady but casual watch on everything she did from morning until the middle of the night. And this was how he discovered something unbelievable. When his wife thought that he wasn't watching, she would cook up a huge amount of rice in the pot. Then, looking around carefully, she would part her hair like a curtain. With this, a huge split would open with a snap at the top of her head. The woman would quickly pour rice into this split, and in the twinkling of an eye, it was all gone.

The man was completely shocked and thought to himself, "So that's it!"

The next morning, the man questioned his wife at length, and his wife answered with a demure face, "Well, oh that?" she said calmly. "That's not me eating, It's a child in my belly asking for more and more, and I give it to him."

"Really? You're having a baby?" Hearing this, the man quickly felt better.

Soon enough, the May festival arrived, and his wife said, "I've been called to my hometown and have to go. After I've heated up the bath and cleaned myself up, I'll be going."

When she had prepared the bath, she called to him, "Listen, as much as I'd like to bathe, it's not right to go in before you, so you go ahead."

"Really? Well, I shouldn't, but . . ."

At the moment the man got in, his wife shouldered the bathtub, with the man still in it, and began to walk outside.

"Hey! Hey! What are you doing?" the man shouted out, in surprise.

"What? It's just that I thought that being inside would be boring, so I wondered how it would be looking at the mountain scenery."

"Ahh, OK, OK. I see." The man was impressed and let himself be jolted along. His wife moved along with rapid strides, deeper and deeper into the mountain, which he thought was strange, and he began to feel a little anxious.

Coming into the depths of the forest, his wife called out to someone, "Heyyy! I've come back now! And look, I've brought a side dish for the festival!"

Hearing this, the man knew he'd been tricked and he felt a chill run down his spine. The color draining from his face and shaking, he grabbed a nearby wisteria vine, leapt away and hid in a thicket. Very quickly Oni demons started appearing from here and there.

"Where's the side dish?"

"Hey! What happened to the side dish?" And they gathered around the wife.

"Look here," the wife said as she put down the bathtub. "It's right here."

"Huh?"

"Where is it?"

When she heard this, the wife looked at the tub, but the man was not there.

"What the . . ." The wife's face suddenly turned into that of a frightening Oni. "Well, he ran away!" And she looked around with eyes aflame.

The man, thinking it would be horrible to be eaten by Oni at such a pass, ran from the thicket in a single breath.

"Hey! He's here. He's here!" A throng of Oni chased after the naked man, pursuing him through the valley and over the mountain, and would not stop. The man was drenched in sweat and his feet were getting tangled in the underbrush, but just as he was resigned to his fate, he spied a tall patch of mugwort growing right there. Running into the middle of it, he found that beneath the mugwort there were a number of irises, and the sharp points of their leaves stuck his eyes. He was about to cry out in pain, but controlled himself, and as he crouched down, the Oni approached.

"Oh! It stinks. There's the stink of a human!"

"Really. What a smell!"

Each one of them thrust its face into the mugwort, one after another, and every one of them had their eyes pierced by the irises. "Oww!" they screamed, their faces twisted in pain. "Aii! This must be a mountain of needles! It's Needle Mountain! Needle Mountain!" With eyes swollen and bright red, they began to run away.

Watching their fleeing figures, the man felt at last that he was going to live.

After that, it is said, the man never wished for such things as a wife that did not eat.

The Note Left by the Demon

Long ago, there was said to be a famous priest at Mount Saku-no-Mae. One day he went to a funeral service and, as he was chanting a sutra, his palms together at the coffin in front of the grave, the sky quickly clouded over. Not only that, but a warm breeze began to blow.

The people gathered together there said, "Well now. What's this? Something bad must be going to happen." And while they commented on what an unusual day it was, rain began to fall.

One person said worriedly, "My, this is very strange. I've heard that in moments like this, an Oni demon will appear," and some began to leave. Nevertheless, the priest continued to chant the sutra.

Just then, something stretched out from the sky and when the people saw this, they all yelled. It was the arm of an Oni with its hand stretched out to touch the funeral casket. At this point, the priest, who had continued to chant the sutra, showed not a hint of flinching, took his prayer beads and slapped the arm with a whack. At that instant, the arm fell down and rolled to the side of the casket. At the same time, the sky that had been so clouded over quickly cleared up and sunlight shone brightly.

Everyone was amazed. "What a great priest!"

"He even struck an Oni's arm!"

Such words of praise went from mouth to mouth, but the priest just nonchalantly wrapped up the Oni's arm in a large kerchief and returned to his temple.

A number of days after that, the priest was chanting a sutra in the main temple hall when a voice called out intently. The priest, however, did not turn around, said, "Wait a while, please," and continued with the sutra. Finally, when he had finished up, he asked "Who is it?" He turned his head and saw a huge Oni standing there.

"Ahh, from the other day . . ." the priest said. "Come in, come in," and going into the interior, took out some cushions and spread them on the floor. The Oni then meekly sat down and, looking at the place of its missing arm, said, "The fact is that I'd like you to return my arm."

"Is that so? Then, why did you do what you did that day?"

"Yes, well, what I did was truly trivial and just on impulse."

"I see, but a human's funeral is a sincere ceremony. There is no excuse for a sudden whim."

"I understand. From now on I'll be more careful."

"But even if I give you back your arm, will you be able to attach it to your body as before?"

"Yes. If I get it back within six days, I can put it back on again. But if I go past that time, it can't be done."

"OK, I understand. I'll give it back to you right away, but please promise that you will never do such evil things again."

"Absolutely. I promise."

Hearing that, the priest left the Oni where it was and sent out a young monk to ask the villagers to all come and gather at the temple. Then, facing the people in the temple garden, he explained everything that had happened up to now.

"In this way, the Oni has apologized. What do you think? I would like you to witness the Oni attaching his arm now. If we do this, the Oni should keep its promise."

He then brought them inside and, in front of all the villagers, took out the Oni's arm that had been secured in a box.

"Ohh! It's that arm . . ."

"Yes! That's it! That's it!"

Voices rang out from here and there.

When the Oni was given back its own arm again, it was overjoyed, and in an instant attached it firmly to its body.

"Well, you did a skillful job of it."

"Yes. Thank you very much. I'll show you the proof of how skillful it was."

So saying, the Oni went down into the garden, lightly lifted up a large rock at the side of the bell hall and brought it in to show them. Hurrahs went up from the crowd.

But one voice was heard to say, "It's great that you're so vigorous, but we'll be troubled if you do evil things again."

Hearing this, the Oni shook its head. "No, I will duly leave you with a proof of my promise."

With that, the young monk brought out paper and red ink. The Oni dipped its hand in the ink and pressed its handprint to the paper. Next to that it wrote, "I will never do evil things again." Then it left.

After that, it is said that the Oni demon never again bothered the villagers.

The Rice Field of the Decapitated Demon

A long time ago, an Oni demon was living in the mountain village of Kashiwadaira. This Oni had a red face and a mouth that split from ear to ear. What's more, he waved his rough and ragged hands about, and when he came down into the village, he committed all sorts of outrageous acts. Everyone was afraid of him, but there was nothing they could do.

For human beings, this Oni was frightening, but among his fellow Oni, he was considered quite normal. It was even said that he received love letters from Momiji, a female Oni in Togakushi.

Well then, hearing the stories about this Oni of Kashiwadaira, a certain general came to defeat it, saying, "I'm going to take care of that Oni." The general, accompanied by his retainers, went to the village and found the Oni.

Yelling, "Hey! Come on!" he began to chase the Oni around and around. As he was an Oni, however, he leapt over a river, pushed his way through a forest, threw aside fleeing children and went through and around the village. But the general managed to catch up with the Oni and with a "Hyaa!" cut off his ear (and even to this day, the people of the village call this place Mimikiri, which means "Cut Ear").

"Ouch! That hurt!" the Oni shouted out in a loud voice, pressing down on the bloody place where his ear had been.

The general continued to chase the Oni, and finally, catching him and holding him down, cut off his head. The villagers were astonished. The general dropped the head into a rice paddy and returned to the capital. After that, this story continued to be circulated among the people of the village, and there were some who felt some sympathy for the Oni.

"It's a shame to leave his head just where it is. We may incur some punishment for that." And with that, a large hole was dug in the center of the village and the head was buried there. There were even people who prayed, "Well then, may he rest in peace."

Nevertheless, there were people who later said, "Listen, an Oni is an evil spirit. It's fine to have such sympathy for this Oni, but if he came back to life, he could take revenge." Because of this, a large stone was then dug out of the mountain and the head was placed on top of it.

"Good enough!" said the villagers.

◊　◊　◊

The rice field where the stone was placed was called "the field of the decapitated Oni." And strangely enough, when you had to step into that rice field for tilling or other work, the next day it inevitably rained. Thus, when people in the village saw that someone had gone into the rice field, they would say, "Today, someone weeded that paddy, so tomorrow it will rain."

But sure enough, as the inevitable rains kept arriving, this situation went beyond strange. Not only the owner of the paddy, but everyone began to be afraid and, making an offering to the priest of the Hojuji, the largest temple in the village, they asked him to till the paddy with his own hands.

"There," thought the villagers. "Everything is all right. The priest has attended to it with the Buddha."

The villagers said such things among themselves, but even after this, if someone stepped into the field, it would rain. It seemed this Oni's influence could not be controlled by human hands.

The Onibaba Demon-Hag
and the Young Girl

A long time ago, an old man and his young granddaughter lived together. One day, the old man went out into the mountains to work. But on leaving, he said to his granddaughter, "All right. Listen carefully. I'm going to lock the door tight. If someone comes, no matter how much they ask for you to open it up, do not do so."

"Yes, Grandpa," the young girl said and, following his instructions, did not go outside and stayed securely inside the house. But shortly, there was the sound of a knock, knock, on the door.

"Who is it?" the young girl asked.

"What are you saying? It's your grandfather. Open the door for a moment, please."

The young girl thought this was strange as her grandfather had just left, and the voice sounded unfamiliar, so she was at a loss of what to do.

"Listen," came the voice, "Open up, please." And again came the knocking at the door. The young girl warily opened the door just a crack and peeped outside. What she saw was a hairy black hand.

"No, you're not my grandfather! I can't open the door!" she said fearfully, and stayed perfectly still. But then, with a scratch and a crunch, someone pushed inside.

It was a terrifying Onibaba demon-hag.

With a "Gyaa!" the young girl ran outside, yelling for her grandfather to help her. But the Onibaba chased after her, screaming for her to wait.

The young girl crossed the Maruki bridge, fled through the forest and hid in a thicket. But the Onibaba clamored,

"The stink of a human! The stink of a human. Where is she! Where is she!"

The young girl turned pale and at last ran out from the thicket. As she ran, she came to a pond where a duck was swimming languidly.

"Duck! Duck, help me!" she cried.

And the duck replied, flapping its wings "Quick! Jump into the pond."

The young girl jumped into the pond as she had been told. Then she saw that she had somehow been turned into a duck herself. With her feet paddling the water, she was able to easily swim away. Just then, the Onibaba arrived and breathing heavily, cocked her head and exclaimed, "How strange. She came this way. But there's still the stink of a human. Maybe she's at the bottom of the pond."

Muttering this, she stuck her head into the pond. At the instant she saw this, the duck pulled the Onibaba's head with all its might, trying to sink the Onibaba to the bottom.

"Ahh! Ahh! This is terrible!" the Onibaba gurgled as she kicked and fought to escape. Realizing that her opponent was the young girl in the form of a duck, she managed to free herself and pounce upon it. But the duck freed itself from the Onibaba's grip and fled from the pond onto the land, where it changed back into the young girl.

"So my eyes weren't crazy after all," said the Onibaba to herself and continued the pursuit. "The stink of a human. I'll be eating soon!" she shouted as she ran.

As the young girl fled from the Onibaba, the two came to a path at the top of a crag. The distance between them had become less and less, and just as the young girl thought that it would soon all be over, she stumbled and fell down. But as the Onibaba approached, she, too, was so exhausted that she tripped over the young girl's body, fell headfirst with a scream off the crag and was killed instantly.

Demons' Day

There is such a thing as Demons' Day, you know.

There were two old men who loved to go fishing more than anything else in the world. One day, the two of them went off to their usual place on the Tenryu River, close to where they lived, carrying a net, but that day they caught not one single fish.

"This is the first time we've come up with nothing," they muttered, but thought that they would try casting their net into the river one more time.

"Keeping trying and don't give up!"

"Hey! We've got something!"

The two men happily pulled the net in to see what they had caught.

"Uh oh! What's this?"

In the middle of the net the head of an Oni demon appeared and it was glaring at them with angry eyes. As you might expect, the two men threw down their net and fled as fast as they could.

"What an extraordinary thing!" they gasped when they'd got as far as a shrine gate on the edge of town and were heaving sighs of relief. As they stood there, they noticed an extraordinarily beautiful woman approaching them. When their eyes met, the woman asked, "Um, did something strange happen today?"

One of the men promptly replied, "You've certainly not guessed far wrong. Something uncanny did happen."

The other man said, "An Oni . . . the head of a huge Oni!"

And just as he was describing what happened, the woman said, "Well, was it something like this?" and her head turned into that of a frightening Oni.

The two men were taken aback and ran away as fast as

they could. Later, when they sat down to rest, they shook their heads in disbelief as they discussed all the things that had happened. And then one of them gave a sudden start—"I've just remembered! Isn't today Demons' Day?"

PART 4

CLUMSY ENCOUNTERS BETWEEN KAPPA AND HUMANS

Kappa Taro

Many years ago, a great number of the water sprites known as Kappa lived here and there throughout the province of Shinano. Among them was a famous Kappa in Lake Megami, which, long ago, was not called Lake Megami, but rather, Akanuma Pond. This stretch of water lay along a path that went from a place called Ashida in the town of Tateshina to Suwa, and the Kappa that lived there was an interesting one.

He was known as Kappa Taro by the local villagers, and when he longed for human company, he would transform himself into a twelve or thirteen-year-old child, and seat himself on top of a rock on the side of the road. He would then call out to anyone who happened to be passing by: "Hey, hey. Won't you pull a hook with me?" and stick out a finger. "Pulling a hook" is a game where you twist a finger with another person and pull with all your might. However, it would be fine if this were just a game, but if someone were carelessly talked into it, the Kappa, who was very strong, would continue pulling hard and in the end, with a jerk, pull his opponent into the lake, submerge and drown that person.

There were many people who were fooled like that and drowned, or so the rumors were in that area.

Well, one day a samurai, Suwa Yorito, who lived in Suwa, heard this rumor, said he was going to defeat this thing and rode his horse to Akanuma Pond with great purpose. Yorito was known for his incredible strength, and when he came up to the aforementioned rock, there was indeed a strange-looking boy sitting atop of it.

"Ah ha! There's Kappa Taro," Yorito thought, watching the Kappa from the corner of his eye.

And sure enough, Kappa Taro stood up, approached the samurai and said, "Hey, hey. Won't you pull a hook with me?"

"Pull a hook? That would be interesting." Yorito answered and, without dismounting, extended a finger. Kappa Taro was unaware of how strong his opponent was and, chuckling, twisted his finger around the samurai's. Just then, Yorito whipped his horse's flank, which set it running. Well, to the Kappa's great surprise, he was pulled along and had to run to keep up.

As Yorito raced his horse down the mountain pass, the Kappa tried to get loose and escape, but there was so much strength in Yorito's finger, it was impossible.

"Oww, oww! That hurts!" the Kappa screamed over and over as he was pulled along. As they went, the Kappa's true form started to reveal itself. Its shell and legs were badly injured and the Kappa was in unbearable pain.

"I give up! I give up! Please forgive me!" the Kappa cried, and begged for its life.

"Huh! Have you understood?" said Yorito. "I came here to punish you for all the evil you've done. So, what do you think? You'll stop doing bad things?"

"Yes! I'll never do such things again. Please forgive me." The horse stopped running and the Kappa put his palms together and lowered his head. And just at that moment, the water in the dish that all Kappa have atop their heads spilled halfway out and the Kappa felt as though its consciousness was growing dim.

Seeing this, Yorito felt sorry for it, dismounted from his horse, scooped up some water in a bamboo tube from the river that was flowing by the side of the road and filled up the saucer. With flowing tears, the Kappa said his thanks and returned to his normal health.

"I'm a Kappa, you know," he said, "and I know many ways of curing human ills. To return the favor of your having spared my life, I will teach them to you."

Yorito listened carefully to the Kappa. And, as the Kappa was about to take its leave, Yorito said, "You have taught me useful things. I will use these techniques to restore people to good health. Nevertheless," he continued, "you have injured many people with the evil you have done. As proof that you have reformed, it would be good if you moved to live somewhere else."

The Kappa hung his head and said, "Yes. For sure."

"Well then, I'll be going!" Yorito manfully whipped his horse and departed.

Kappa Taro, now left behind, sat on the rock at the side of Akanuma Pond and muttered disconsolately, "Ahh, ah. Now I'll be leaving this place." Yet, he could not imagine a good place where he might go.

But then at some point, the scenery of Nonoiri that he had once seen floated into his head. Nonoiri, now the town of Nagawa, is a peaceful place at the foot of the highlands of Utsukushigahara.

Although he was struck with this idea, he couldn't decide whether to make a move or stay where he was. But during the night, he moved the water of the Akanuma Pond along with its fish to Nonoiri. And, thereupon, a lake suddenly appeared at a place where there wasn't anything like one before and the villagers came out to look at it in great surprise.

In the end, this lake became known as Yonoike, which means "night lake," and is still there today.

The Kappa and the Dumplings

Long ago there was a cute baby boy born into the house of a village headman. A single beggar was sleeping beneath the veranda of a shrine. Suddenly . . .

"Yaa! Yaa!" a clamorous voice could be heard from outside. "Is the shrine god here?"

"Oh my! What a surprise to see you, Hachiman, God of Oracles!" the shrine god responded. "Why are you here?"

"A child was born in the house of the headman today and I have come to take it."

"Ah! This is so unfortunate," the shrine god said, with seeming regret. "I have a guest and can't go along. Pardon me this once."

Without the assistance of the local shrine god, there was nothing to be done, so Hachiman made to leave. But then the shrine god called after him.

"Sorry for all your trouble. This child that was born—what was it?"

"It was a male."

"How long will it live?"

"Until it is seven years old."

"How will it die?"

"It will be swept away in a river and drown."

"And what day?"

"On the eleventh day of the eleventh month."

The beggar heard this entire conversation and wondered what he should do as he walked around and finally arrived in front of the headman's house where a great celebration was going on due to the birth of the aforementioned son. When the red-faced headman saw this shabbily dressed man, however, he formally and cheerfully invited him to come in for a drink. But the beggar, troubled by what he had just heard, did not feel like opening his mouth. He did not reach for the sake nor did he eat the delicacies offered.

♦ ♦ ♦

Well then, seven years passed and finally the eleventh day of the eleventh month arrived. The beggar was worried, called in at the house of the village headman and fully disclosed what he had heard that day.

"Where is the child now?" he asked timidly.

The headman was horribly shocked and gathered together everyone in his mansion.

"Listen up!" he exclaimed in great agitation. "The boy told me that he wanted to go fishing at the river, and went out. He said he would keep fishing until the afternoon and would come home then, so I gave him some rice dumplings with bean jam to take along. But I have no idea where he went, so everyone, go look for him quickly!"

Just as the house was thrown into great confusion, the boy returned, looking terrified.

"Ahh, a scary thing happened to me today," he said.

And according to his story, he had gone to the deep Momiji Pond, cast his line, and a strange-looking boy with staring eyes and dressed in Buddhist robes had emerged from the middle of the pond.

"What are you doing?" the strange-looking boy asked.

"I'm fishing," the headman's son responded.

This was just about the time he was starting to feel hungry, and without further ado, he sat down and began eating the dumplings he had brought along. But it occurred to him that eating them by himself was not right and offered some to the strange-looking boy, saying that he had a lot more.

The strange-looking boy then devoured the dumplings as though they were quite delicious, before abruptly bursting into tears.

"I'm not a real human being," he confessed. "I'm a Kappa water sprite, and I always drag people into the river, take out their livers and eat them. But today I received your kind gift and therefore I will refrain."

So saying, he sank into the pool and disappeared.

Everyone was astonished to hear the story and gave great shouts of joy.

"Well, you were saved thanks to the rice dumplings with bean jam!" they said, expressing their gratitude to the dumplings. And now, to this day in this village, if people are serving these dumplings at home, they will cast some into the river, and no one has ever drowned there since.

The Kappa's Wonderful Medicine

Long ago, near the Otagiri River in the area of Ina, there lived a landowner by the name of Nakamura Shinroku. Shinroku was an official for the Takato clan and his duty was to oversee the timber that was floated down the Tenryu River.

One summer day, Shinroku had been washing his horse, when someone sitting on a nearby rock, wiping the sweat from his body, muttered, "My, how hot it is today."

Just at that moment, the horse, which was tied to a tree, began to whinny and become restive.

"Here, here! What's the matter?" Shinroku called out, and saw that a Kappa water sprite had its hands on the horse's flanks and was pulling it vigorously toward the river.

"Yaa!" Just as Shinroku hurriedly ran to its side, the horse shook loose its rope and, stumbling up the riverbank, ran off at full speed. Shinroku chased after the horse, which had the Kappa hanging onto its tail, but soon lost sight of it.

Well then, a while after that, a laborer was mowing the grass in the garden at Shinroku's house when he thought he heard a horse neighing, and sure enough, the horse ran up to him. The laborer thought this was suspicious and wondered what had happened to Shinroku.

Seizing the horse, he put it into a shed for the moment.

"Come now, where have you put my master?" the laborer asked, looking at the horse, but of course it didn't answer. Then, thinking that it would not do to have the horse go hungry, he filled some pails with grass and water.

"A horse cannot speak, so this is a problem," he said and was just about to leave the shed when a head suddenly appeared from inside one of the pails. "What the . . ." he thought, and when he looked more closely, there was a Kappa, grinning at him.

"Why you!" the laborer yelled, and quickly pulled it up by the neck. "You came here to do more evil, I'll bet!" And with that, he tied it up with a rope.

Soon thereafter, Shinroku returned, breathing hard, and seeing the Kappa, said in surprise, "Ah, you scoundrel! So you have come here."

He then told the laborer what had happened, and in the end, the laborer said, "Master, if we just leave him tied up like this, he'll surely escape and do more evil. What do you think? Shall we just cut off its head?"

When it heard this, the Kappa turned pale and started to cry. Then it turned to Shinroku. "Master," it said with its eyes spilling tears, "Please just spare my life. I'll never do anything bad from this moment on."

Seeing this, Shinroku felt sorry for the creature and asked repeatedly, "Well then, will you promise?"

"Yes! For sure!"

Hearing this, Shinroku had the laborer untie the rope. The Kappa shivered with relief and said, "Thank you. In return for your having been kind enough to spare me, I will teach you how to make a medicine that will cure any illness."

"A medicine?"

Yes. If you use this medicine when you have pains in the joints of your hands and feet, you will get relief right away."

"Oh. A medicine for gout?"

Shinroku was half in doubt, but wrote down on a piece of paper what the Kappa told him. When he had finished writing, he said, "I see," nodded his head and returned the Kappa to the river.

◊   ◊   ◊

After that, Shinroku took out the paper many times and tried the medicine in the way the Kappa had explained. As a test, he thought he would try it on the old lady afflicted with gout who was staying at the house of some relatives. The medicine was so effective that people couldn't stop praising Shinroku.

"This is the wonderful medicine the Kappa taught us how to make." This story spread from village to village and the name of Nakamura Shinroku became famous in no time for his Kappa's wonderful medicine. And it is said that from then on, there was always a line of visitors patiently waiting outside Shinroku's house.

PART 5

WHEN TENGU STILL LIVED AMONG US

No Match for the Tengu
of Mount Minakami

There have been various lords of Matsushiro Castle, and among them was a lord by the name of Tamaru who had no sense of faith or belief at all. He never went to pray at shrines or temples, which made his retainers uneasy; and maybe his lack of faith was the reason why the young princess born to him had not grown teeth even when she had reached the age of thirteen. Tamaru worried about this and thought that if this situation continued, the princess would never be able to find a husband.

One day, when he was feeling particularly resentful about this problem with his daughter, he suddenly said, "Tomorrow we're going hunting on Mount Minakami. Prepare your bows and arrows."

Mount Minakami was to the east of the town of Matsushiro, and gave one a sense of tranquility, looking like soft protruding buttocks. But everyone was surprised at this command because the mountain was considered a holy place, the home of a Tengu goblin, and no one went hunting there.

When his retainers reminded him about the Tengu, the lord replied, "Ha ha ha! What? A Tengu? What impudence! Just what is a Tengu? If it were to show itself to me, I'd easily defeat it with my arrows. So let's go up and hunt on the mountain. No one goes there, so there will be plentiful game, and when we come back we'll have a big drinking party with lots of sake and song!"

Well then, the next day the lord took along his retainers and headed for the mountain. As they were climbing its slopes, they disturbed a flock of pheasants that flew up into the air with a rustling sound.

"Hey! Bring them down! What are you waiting for?" commanded the lord, irritated that his retainers were hesitating.

One of the retainers said, "My lord, we should really not do this. Please . . ."

And other retainers added, "What will we do if there is punishment for this?" and so on.

The lord spoke to a falconer that he had brought along for the occasion: "You have always obediently stood by the things that I say." And then he commanded, "Send out your falcon to catch a pheasant!"

"Yes," the falconer said. And following his lord's command, he released the falcon, which immediately caught a pheasant and came back. Both the lord and the falconer were overjoyed and, repeating this again and again, soon filled up a basket with pheasants.

Then, just as they released the falcon one more time, a huge shadow spread above their heads, turning the place dark as night.

"What! What is this?"

The men gathered together and raised their voices, but at the same time, the huge shadow took the form of an eagle and, spreading its wings, pounced upon the falcon. Gripping the falcon, it carried it to the branch of a pine tree where it tore the falcon to pieces with its beak. The falcon's wings fell piteously to the ground bit by bit, and when the lord saw this, he yelled impatiently, "Ah! This detestable eagle! Quickly, bring it down! Guns! Use your guns!"

But the eagle was not affected by bullets at all, and even though it was hit, did not fall, but rather flew off leisurely to the eastern sky.

As they all watched it go, their hearts turned cold. "That was surely a Tengu in the form of an eagle," one man said. Others spoke together and agreed.

And one man said tearfully, "We're surely going to receive some punishment soon. We're going to die."

Hearing this, the lord said with a show of courage, "That's all right. Just leave it to me," but was also frightened himself.

With a "That's enough for today. Let's go back to the castle," they quickly went down the mountain.

◊   ◊   ◊

After that, the lord withdrew to the interior of the castle and did not show his face to his retainers. Seven days passed. Finally he appeared at his desk, seeming as though he had made a decision, and wrote a letter:

> I am Tamaru, the protector of Matsushiro Castle. Recently, when I went hunting, everyone said that a Tengu appeared in the form of an eagle. But if it truly was a Tengu, would you please have my princess grow the teeth of a normal person by tomorrow? If you can do this, I will have faith in the Tengu and pay homage to it. Then, if you give her teeth, I will plant one cedar tree for each tooth at the shrine. If my request is not fulfilled, I will judge that believing in the Tengu has no value, and destroy all the temples and shrines on Mount Minakami.

Having written this up, he called his retainers and said, "All right. Today, I want you to take this letter, place it at the shrine on the top of the mountain and then come back."

The day soon came to an end, night passed and then the dawn broke. The lord was impatient to see whether his request had been granted, and called for the princess.

"Well now, open your mouth. Ahh."

The princess did as she was told, and there were the teeth, grown all in a line. The lord was overjoyed. In a single night, beautiful white shining teeth had appeared just as he had asked. Seeing this, the lord, as lord he was, not only had faith in the Tengu, but also worshipped the gods and buddhas with great care.

And of course, he planted the cedar trees he had promised at the shrine on the mountain.

The Old Man and the Tengu's Child

In a certain village, there was an old lady who had died before her time, and her old man passed his days in sorrow. But even then, he did his work as a woodcutter, cutting firewood. Every day he would take his ax and climb the nearby mountain.

One day, he was resting against a tree stump, wishing, as he often did, that he could see a beautiful fireworks display lighting up the heavens where his wife now resided. Just then, he heard someone calling "Old man, old man!" Right before him appeared a child with a long nose and a red face.

When the old man looked carefully, wasn't that the ax that he always carried now in the child's hand? "Ahh," he lamented, "If that child takes my ax, I cannot be a woodcutter at all."

Then the child said, as though he understood the old man at the bottom of his heart, "Old man, do you long for the old lady that much?" At that, the old man looked yet again, and thought that this was not an ordinary child, and just might be the child of a Tengu goblin.

"Yes, that's right! I am a Tengu's child," said the boy, reading the old man's mind and handing him back the ax. "And I've cut all the wood for you."

He then took the old man to a place a little farther away and when the old man looked, he saw that a lot of firewood had been piled up.

"Well now!" the old man exclaimed. "You've been quite helpful. You really put yourself into this!"

"No, it was nothing," the Tengu's child replied.

"Well then, would you be kind enough to come back tomorrow?" the old man asked cheerfully, feeling as though he had gained a child.

"Yes," said the Tengu's child, and flew away happily.

After that, the Tengu's child came every day and helped with cutting firewood, and together they would eat the rice balls the old man brought.

When they had nearly brought the work of woodcutting in that place to an end, the old man asked, "Will you be kind enough to continue coming?"

"Of course I will. Now I think you would like to see some fireworks," the child said, and when the man nodded in surprise, continued, "The Omi autumn festival is in three days time, and they'll be having a display. I'll take you there."

However, Omi was far away and the old man would not be able to make it on foot. Thinking this over, the Tengu's child said, "Well then, I'll come again in three days," and flew off to the top of a nearby tree before disappearing deep into the mountain forest.

♦　　♦　　♦

The old man happily waited for that day to come. When three days had passed, he was resting against a tree stump when a voice shouted from above, "Old man! Old man!"

Looking up, there was the Tengu's child perched in the branches above him.

"Well, well," said the old man. "You came. Thank you!"

The Tengu's child placed the old man on his back and in no time they came to the Omi festival, where fireworks were being sent up into the sky. The two sat together on a rock.

"Ahh, how beautiful!"

"Look!"

"They're so big!"

The two enjoyed the display together and the Tengu's child said, "Old man, are you happy that you saw this beautiful fireworks display lighting up the heavens where your wife now lives?"

"Yes, I am," the old man said. But when he looked to his side, he saw that the Tengu's child had suddenly disappeared. Thinking this to be strange, he walked back to his house; but the road, which he thought to be so long, was no trouble at all. Even stranger, when he got back to the house, there was the Tengu's child seated on the veranda waiting for him.

"That was good, wasn't it, old man." So saying, the Tengu's child poured him a cup of sake from a gourd. And after that, they say, the old man became extraordinarily healthy and lived to be a hundred years old.

The Tengu's Night Watch

Speaking of Tengu goblins, a number of them of great size were rumored to live in the Atera Valley deep in the Kiso Mountains. What might have been called their function seemed to have been to punish people who had come from other places to damage the mountains, and they often walked around the mountains keeping a lookout.

Well, unaware of this, a man came from elsewhere, intending to help himself to some firewood. "I've never seen anyone this deep in the mountains," he said, "so I'll shoulder a large bundle and go home."

With this, he took a sickle and was cutting some branches, when, as he paused for a moment, a huge hand stretched out from behind and tightened around his body.

"Hey! What's going on? Wha . . . Who is it?" As he shouted out in a loud voice, the man was hauled up so high into the sky that he could see the valley far below him.

"Huh! I'll teach you!"

And just as he heard this said, the man's body fell down into the valley in an instant and was smashed and broken to pieces. At the same time, the loud laughing voice of a Tengu resounded through the mountain. "What do you think about that then? Did you learn your lesson? Outsiders who come to lay waste to the mountain get this kind of treatment."

◊　◊　◊

The rumor that a Tengu lived on that particular mountain became widespread, and two young men from the village, who worked as grass cutters, wanting to see something scary, decided to go there one night.

"They say such things about this, but we'll just have to see it with our own eyes." The next morning they started to do some mowing. The two had cut only a bit of grass when they began to look around restlessly wondering where the Tengu might be.

"If it appears, I'm going to cut off its long nose, take it home and show it off to everyone."

"Ahh, while you take the nose, I'll take its fan, kick it around and everyone will have a great time."

They talked together like this as they ate their lunch.

After a while, they became impatient and called out without any sense of fear, "Hey! Tengu! If you're there, come on out now!"

Finally, the sun went down and the place gradually darkened. And though it was summer, the air became cold. The two snuggled down to rest into the grass they had cut. Nevertheless, if they went to sleep now, they would have not attained their goal. Lying there awake, they continued to wait for the Tengu to appear. But even though the stars began to twinkle in the sky, there was no sign of a Tengu.

"What now? Are we going to go back like this without seeing anything at all?"

"What was the point of bothering to come here?"

But just as they were whispering such things to each other, a strange sound of footsteps came from far away.

Doshin! Doshin!

And as the two looked at each other, there was another sound coming closer and closer, like someone blowing into a conch shell.

Bo! Bo!

"I think it's come!"

As might be expected, the two were terrified and they burrowed deep into the grass they had gathered. Straining their ears, they could hear the footsteps right next to them. Then, suddenly, the grass covering them was swept away and the faces of two Tengu appeared, looking down at the two shaking men.

"Do you believe in us now?" they laughed. "We Tengu go

around the mountain on night watch like this," and together they blew conch shells and waved their pilgrim staffs.

"Ah, noble Tengu, we believe in you, we believe in you! From the bottom of our hearts, we will never doubt you again. Please forgive us!"

The two men put their palms to the earth and apologized. Seeing that, the Tengu laughed out loud and stepped away. *Doshin! Doshin!*

The two men hurriedly ran down the mountain and told the villagers what they had seen that night. People then became more respectful of the mountain and grateful to the Tengu as well.

The Chestnut Tree
Training Hall of the Tengu

The neighborhood of Ono in the town of Shiogiri was full of trees that bore nothing but small chestnuts. But if the chestnuts were small, the branches of the trees were laden with them and these trees were called "Honorable Tengu." This was the place where Tengu goblin children would mostly go for training.

A long, long time ago, when the trees were full of new chestnuts, the Tengu children would hang from the trees, practice flying from branch to branch and walk all over the sharp chestnuts. But many of the Tengu children treated the trees roughly and, as you might suspect, the trees were injured and had no time to produce proper nuts. Nowadays, the Tengu no longer go there.

"Hey! Fly with more spirit! Come on now! This time try flying up toward the sky!"

The voice of the Tengu who was teaching the children used to echo through the area like this every day.

The Tengu of Mount Taro

Today, the people of the town of Ueda do not believe the stories of a Tengu goblin living on nearby Mount Taro, but it seems that, indeed, there was one living there.

Long ago, this Tengu walked with heavy strides from Mount Asama, stepped onto Mount Taro and quickly ascended to its peak.

"Oh! Oh!" it exclaimed, as it staggered awkwardly, bracing its fingers on the earth. (It is said that these footprints and fingerprints clearly remain to this day, and the names attached to them are "The Footprints Crevice" and "The Finger-Struck Crevice." Even today, grass and trees do not grow there and it's all a bit strange.)

Well then, the Tengu that came to Mount Taro felt that the view was so splendid, and that the shape of the mountain and its comfortableness were so fine, that it laughed and declared it an excellent place. It then sat down and was determined to make this mountain its home. The beautiful Chiguma River flowed through the landscape below, there were the figures of people working in the Ueda basin, the peaceful aspect of the villages could be seen, and even the breeze felt good. This was just at the time of rice-planting, and all the villagers were working diligently in the paddies.

"What?" the Tengu thought. "Even the children are working hard!"

Just as the Tengu was gazing down and thinking these thoughts, it let out a great snore and fell asleep. After a while, it woke up.

"Huh?" it exclaimed and rubbed its eyes in disbelief. In what had just now been a scene of rice-planting, the entire area was completely planted and had changed into beautiful rice fields.

"Well, well. I have to give it to them. These people are second to none." And his eyes grew big and round.

◊　◊　◊

In this way, the Tengu of Mount Taro became a good-natured and gentle Tengu, but would become very angry at people's evil deeds. Because of this, when it identified a person who had committed evil among those who climbed Mount Taro to look out at the scenery, it would kick that evil person and send them tumbling off the mountain.

One day, when the Tengu was resting in its customary pine tree, a man came along, "Oh," he said, "this tree has fine branches. I'll cut one and take it home," and began to do just that. But before he could begin, he stumbled backwards and fell down a ravine to his death.

Thus, it was clear that the Tengu would look carefully at what people did and would punish the evil ones.

But this is a story from long, long ago.

The Child Who Became a Tengu

Long ago, there were any number of stories about children being kidnapped by Tengu goblins, but you didn't hear stories about children who lived in villages turning into Tengu. But this is such a story—from a village in Azumidaira in the foothills of Mount Ariake—and surprisingly, is said to have actually happened.

In this village there was a man by the name of Kyube, who had an only son, Shintaro. One day, Shintaro went off with three friends, leading a horse, heading to Mount Ariake to gather bamboo grass. Shooing away wasps from the horse's nose, they journeyed on, but as they got closer to the mountain Shintaro's facial features gradually turned scary. And suddenly, he nimbly flew up from the horse's back where he had been sitting, and alighted on a crag as though he had sprouted wings.

"What's going on with you?" his companions said in surprise. "Come down right now."

But he did not come down, and it was not only that. As they looked, they could see that his legs were gradually lengthening and increasing in size and his head seemed to reach the clouds.

The children looking on were so shocked that they collapsed onto the ground. And just then, Shintaro's body disappeared into the clouds, leaving only his legs visible. And from the clouds, thunder could be heard.

Just as they thought they could hear a voice saying, "Bye-bye! So long!" the long legs began to move, striding toward the valley, and disappearing into Mount Ariake.

Shintaro's companions stood there in amazement. In the distance they momentarily heard the sound of breaking rocks and large trees falling. But then everything became quiet.

The children finally came back to their senses, and, greatly agitated, ran home yelling, "Shintaro! Shintaro!"

After they had told everyone what had happened, the villagers discussed the matter together, declaring that Shintaro must have turned into a Tengu, and expressing their sympathy for Kyube.

Kyube mourned for his only son after this and even when the season came to plant the rice seedlings, looked off in the direction of Mount Ariake with tears in his eyes.

At last, the mountains were covered with green and the season for rice-planting was over. Kyube's paddies, however, were left bare among the others.

"This is troubling," the villagers thought, as they looked at Kyube's paddies and worried for him. Talking it over, they decided to help him out with planting the rice seedlings.

But, one morning, Kyube got up tearfully and went out to look at his rice paddies.

"Wha . . . what's this?" he cried out in shock. Overnight, the paddies had been planted with green seedlings that now swayed in the cool breeze. Kyube wondered who had helped him and went about questioning the villagers, but not a single person said that this was their work.

Everyone wondered at this strange thing until at last, the autumn winds began to blow. Kyube's rice grew rapidly and his paddies were even more full of life than those of his neighbors. As the rice ears began to droop, his rice fields were now the best in the village.

Everyone praised him endlessly, but thought, "This is great, but how will one man be able to harvest all this rice?" And then again, a something odd occurred. In one single night, all of the rice was cut and stacked. The villagers wondered how this could have happened.

Then someone said, "Come to think of it, late last night I heard a strange rumbling sound coming from the direction of the mountain."

After that, the same thing happened every year, and eventually one of the villagers declared, "Well now, this must be the act of Shintaro, who turned into a Tengu, feeling sympathy for his father."

Kyube agreed and, often turning toward Mount Ariake and placing his palms together, gave thanks to the son who became a Tengu.

PART 6

YAMAMBA MOUNTAIN WITCHES

The Yamamba and the Cattle Herder

When one hears the name Sanjuro, a hardworking man comes to mind. This is because people used to see him every day, leading an ox or riding on its back, the ox always loaded with salt and fish he had bought in the seaside villages of Echigo. These things that he had purchased, he sold to villagers in the mountains.

Now one day Sanjuro was returning home with his ox, carrying packages of dried cod and other fish, when suddenly a Yamamba mountain witch appeared in front of him.

"Hey. Give me two of your codfish," she demanded.

Sanjuro was surprised, but kept calm. "No, I won't," he replied and led his ox off to the side.

At this, the Yamamba said, "What! Don't you know how dreadful I can be? You'll pay for this! I'll eat both you and your ox!" And her eyes began to sparkle.

Sanjuro was frightened and there was nothing he could do, and so he threw two dried codfish to the Yamamba. She gobbled them down in the twinkling of an eye.

"Sanjuro! Sanjuro!" she kept calling, but Sanjuro jumped on the ox's back, whipped its flanks and rode off quickly, gasping for breath.

But the Yamamba chased after him, yelling, "One more! One more!"

Her face was frightening and appeared to be as red as fire, so, not knowing what else to do, Sanjuro threw her one more dried codfish and fled. Still, the Yamamba chased after him. "Give me more! If you don't, I'll eat both you and your ox!"

With this, Sanjuro was all the more terrified, threw down the package of codfish and rode away.

Her mouth watering, the Yamamba untied the package and, murmuring, "Ah, how delicious! How delicious," ate the dried codfish all up. However, she then continued the chase.

"I'm still hungry," she called after him. "Well, there's nothing for it, so I'll eat your ox." Rolling her eyes, which had grown yellow, she chased Sanjuro on and on.

Thinking that if this situation continued, he would be eaten too, Sanjuro abandoned the ox and ran. But when the Yamamba had eaten the ox, she continued to pursue Sanjuro. Running desperately, Sanjuro came to a large pine tree standing at the side of a swamp and, in a panic, scrambled up as high as he could. Then, as he held his breath, the Yamamba came to the tree and went around and around it.

"Sanjuro!" she called out. "Sanjuro! Where are you? Ah, he must be hiding in there . . ." Seeing Sanjuro's reflection in the swamp water, she confidently waded in.

"Aha! Sanjuro! Don't run away!" Grasping at the shimmering reflection, her efforts were fruitless again and again. Meanwhile, Sanjuro silently climbed down from the tree, fled through a thicket and ran for his life. As he ran, he came to a solitary house and rushed inside.

After a while, the Yamamba entered the house. "Well now, It smells like there's a human being in my house. Someone must be here," and she looked restlessly about the place. Sanjuro shook with fear as he held on tight to the beams of the ceiling. He had had no idea that this was the house of the Yamamba.

Below him, the Yamamba muttered, "Huh! How regrettable! If I had eaten Sanjuro, how tasty he would have been." And, lighting a fire in the hearth, she started to heat up a large piece of mochi rice cake, which swelled up nicely. But the Yamamba was so tired out that she unwittingly fell asleep.

Sanjuro laughed to himself, and pulling a stalk of miscanthus from the underside of the thatched roof, quietly reached out with its tip, speared the mochi and pulled it toward him. When he ate it, how delicious it was!

When the Yamamba awoke, the mochi was gone.

"Oh no! My mochi has been eaten up! Who was it?" she grumbled, and looked vacantly around.

"The one who ate it was the fire god," whispered Sanjuro, in a disguised voice. "Ahh, how good it was."

"What? The fire god?" the Yamamba said meekly. "Well then, there's no reason to be angry." And she then hung a pot over the hearth and began to warm some sweet sake. As the sweet sake began to emit a fragrant smell, the Yamamba again fell asleep.

When Sanjuro saw that this had happened again, he lowered a hollow stick of miscanthus and sucked the sweet sake through its opening.

When the Yamamba awoke, she shouted, "Oh no! Where did my sweet sake go?"

"The one who drank it was the fire god," Sanjuro said in the same voice as before.

"The fire god? Ah, it was the fire god. Well, there's nothing to be done," the Yamamba muttered. "I guess I'll go to sleep. So where shall I sleep tonight?" And she looked around. There were two storage chests: one made of wood, the other made of stone. Rice containers had been put inside both of them.

Sanjuro then said in his same disguised voice, "The wooden one. The wooden one."

"If the fire god says the wooden one, that's what I'll do," she responded, and opened up the chest, shut the lid and began to fall asleep.

Without hesitation, Sanjuro climbed down one of the pillars, put some water in the pot and heated it until it started to bubble noisily.

The Yamamba asked sleepily, "What's that bubbling?"

"A bubbling bird has come," Sanjuro answered.

"Really? Really? What a pleasant sound," the Yamamba said.

Sanjuro put more wood onto the fire, which began to make a crackling sound.

"What's that crackling sound?" the Yamamba asked.

"The crackling bird has come," Sanjuro answered again.

"Really? Really? What a pleasant sound," the Yamamba said yet again.

Meanwhile the bubbling water began to boil fiercely and

Sanjuro took a drill and opened up a hole in the wooden chest.

"What's that drilling sound?"

"The drilling bird has come."

"Really? Really? What a pleasant sound."

Just as the Yamamba was saying this, Sanjuro poured the boiling water from the pot into the hole in the chest.

"Oww! Oww!" the Yamamba screamed, and she died on the spot.

Sanjuro opened the chests and, to his surprise, they were full of gold coins. Taking them home, he bought a large ox and continued his work trading salt and fish.

The Yamamba's Gourd

At the word "Yamamba," one can only think of an evil being, but there are also Yamamba mountain witches that are easygoing. And this story is about one such easygoing Yamamba. This one particular Yamamba carried a strange gourd and often would buy sake when in a village. The gourd that she carried was quite small.

One day the Yamamba went into the sake shop of a village she was passing through and asked the owner to fill up her gourd with ten quarts of sake.

"There no way I could fill up such a small gourd with ten quarts [nine liters] of sake," the sake shop owner said.

But the Yamamba just chuckled, "Now, now. No need to worry," and paid no attention to him.

There was nothing for it, so the shop owner poured the sake gurgling into the gourd, and though it looked as though it would only have held a little over a pint, all ten quarts went right in.

Now this area was suffering a long dry spell and the villagers were suffering and praying for water, water, water.

"There's not even enough water for the babies to drink."

"How much longer will this child live?"

Such sad words were being spoken, but when dawn broke, the villagers who went to the shrine to pray were astonished. In front of the worship hall, small gourds were lined up closely together.

"What . . . what's this?" someone exclaimed.

"Ahh. These gourds are just like the one the Yamamba always carries around," another man said. When they picked up the gourds and shook them, they could feel water swishing around inside.

"Aha! Just as I thought!"

Everyone divided up the gourds and took them home. When they poured them into water jars, the jars quickly filled to the point of overflowing.

With this, the villagers were saved and every year with the coming of summer, they would show their gratitude to the Yamamba by holding a festival in her honor.

The Sake-Buying Yamamba

In a certain village, there was a sake shop on the east and a sake shop on the west. The sake shop on the east was run by an unselfish man and his wife, and they didn't have much money. The sake shop on the west was run by an avaricious husband and wife, and they were rich.

Well now, this happened one night as the year was drawing to an end. A miserable old lady with long disheveled hair came to the sake shop on the east.

"It's so cold, I'd like to drink some sake and sleep," she said to the man at the counter, and held out a small sake bottle.

"Certainly," the man replied pleasantly, for he had no reason to think there was anything unusual about someone coming in to buy sake.

"Fill it up with about three quarts," the old lady said.

"What?" The sake seller exclaimed. "Old woman, will it hold three quarts?"

"Yes, it certainly will," she said with a serious expression.

Though thinking this was a bit strange, the man poured the sake into the small bottle, and with a glug, glug, glug, sure enough, it was just as the old lady had said.

"Well now! This is quite a surprise," said the proprietor, rubbing the sake bottle and inspecting it thoroughly. But there was no sign of a leak.

"Three quarts," the old lady said calmly. "Well then, I'll pay the bill and be off." And this she did.

The proprietor called in his wife and counted the money over and over, but it was absolutely the correct price. "Maybe these are forgeries?" he wondered, holding the bills with which she had paid him under a lamp.

"If you doubt your customers like that, you'll never prosper," his wife cautioned.

"You're right," the sake seller said with embarrassment, and that night went to sleep feeling full of remorse.

◊   ◊   ◊

After that, the next night and the next, when the old lady came back to buy anything from two to four quarts of sake, she would pay the correct price and go home.

But the old lady did not just go to this shop to buy sake. She also went to the sake shop on the west, and in the same way, appeared there to buy sake at night. And in the same way, she brought a small sake bottle and asked the proprietor to fill it up with four or six quarts of sake. Then she would pay the correct price and go home. When the proprietor remarked that she was a strange customer, his wife said, "Whether you pour four or six quarts in that bottle, it's filled up, isn't it? When she asks for six quarts, why not just stop pouring at two?" and urged him to cheat her in this way.

"Yes, good idea," he concurred, and the next day did just that. Without noticing what the proprietor had done, the old lady thanked him, paid the correct price and went home. The man's wife said, "I taught you a good trick. What do you think? Maybe I should teach you how to run this business."

"You're right."

"This is what business is all about."

After that, the old lady kept going to the sake shop on the east and the sake shop on the west, but one day she suddenly stopped coming.

Nevertheless, the poor sake shop on the east now prospered, while no customers came to the sake shop on the west and it went bankrupt.

Among the villagers, it was rumored that the old lady was indeed a Yamamba mountain witch and that she had perhaps been testing the sincerity of the two shops.

The Man-Eating Yamamba

Long ago, there were two children—an older brother and a younger sister—who lost their mother at an early age and so were brought up by a stepmother.

The stepmother was an ill-tempered woman who did not treat the children with any tenderness at all. "How relieved I would be if these children were to die," she thought, and wondered what she should do.

Then one day, after pondering this matter . . .

"I'm going to the mountains to relax today. You come along, too," she said; and taking the children along, went quickly deep into the mountains. After a while, they came to a dilapidated hut.

"Well, let's go inside and warm up with a fire. I'll go get some firewood." So doing, she lit a fire in the hearth. "Stay here," she said to the children. "I'll be back soon."

Yet, she did not return, even when it grew dark. And this was, of course, because she had returned home.

"Ahh, I'm finally free of having to worry about those children," she thought, and comfortably ate a nice meal.

Meanwhile, the brother and sister had given up on waiting. They left the hut and tried to find their own way home through the mountains. But somehow, they lost their way and, no matter how long they walked, they were unable to see the lights of the village.

They were becoming forlorn and numb with cold. But just as they thought they were lost forever, they saw a light coming from a small, crude little hut.

"There's nothing else for it, we'll have to ask for help at that house," the elder brother said. The two children knocked at the door of the hut and a white-haired old lady came out and chuckled as she heard their story.

"Well, well, you poor little things." Bringing them inside, she had them eat a meal. This old lady, however, was a man-eating Yamamba mountain witch, and from the moment she saw these children, she wanted terribly to eat them.

"Well, I'll fatten them up a little first," she thought, and deciding to eat the older brother first, shut him up in the back of the hut. Thinking that she would eat the younger sister after setting her to work, she gave the little girl various chores to do.

◊   ◊   ◊

The days passed . . .

"By and by, I should go ahead and eat that child," the Yamamba thought to herself. She took the older brother out of the hut and began to lick him with her tongue. To the younger sister, she said, "All right. I'm going to boil and eat this kid now, so fill that big cauldron with water and light up a fire."

Hearing this, the little sister shook all over and didn't know what to do.

"Uhh . . ." She tried to think of something to say that would save her brother, but the Yamamba said coolly, "Don't you know how to light a fire? Here, let me," and did it herself.

The little sister stood and watched as the water in the cauldron was brought to a boil.

The Yamamba grabbed the older brother and dragged him toward the cauldron, when the boy said, "Ahh, I can get in by myself, but could you show me the best way to do it?"

"What? You don't know how to get in?" the old woman laughed. "Look! Like this," and she positioned herself as though she was about to jump in headfirst. Just then someone pushed the Yamamba from behind and she immediately fell in.

"Ooww!" she screamed, but the brother and sister quickly put the lid on the cauldron and that was the end of the Yamamba. The children hugged each other in happiness. After

that, they packed all sorts of rare things that were in the hut into a bag.

"This time, we're going home and we won't get lost!"

"Right!"

They walked along the road that led from the witch's house and before long came to a river that they knew. They needed to cross the river but there was no bridge there and they did not know what to do. But just then, two ducks flew up out of nowhere.

"Ah! These are the ducks that we keep at the house." As the older brother said this in surprise, the ducks became bigger and bigger, took the two children on their backs and brought them home.

At the house, the stepmother was shocked to see the two. She had never imagined that the children she had abandoned would return like this. They happily and innocently took out all the rare things they had brought back with them and showed her. She, of course, felt ashamed at what she had done and recovered a feeling of tenderness toward them.

"My goodness, how nice," she sighed. "All these gifts!"

From that time on, the desire to abandon the children never ever arose again.

The Yamamba Gets Angry

One day, a shabby woman no one had seen before came to a village and said, "I can work in the rice fields, do needlework or anything, so please hire me to do something."

The villagers thought she had a sinister look and, as she did not tell them where she had come from, they did not take her on. But there was one man who felt sorry for her, built a crude hut where she could stay on the outskirts of the village, and had her weed his vegetable garden. He was surprised at how quickly and neatly she finished the work and couldn't believe she had done everything all by herself.

Many of the others who found out about this, then made requests for her to harvest their rice. The woman graciously accepted but when the villagers asked how they should pay her, she replied, "Well, if you'll just feed me, that will be payment enough."

At this simple answer, everyone asked her to do job after job. At any rate, when she was asked to cut and bring in firewood from the mountain to burn during the winter, and she did this job in a single day although it would ordinarily have taken three, the villagers were understandably astonished. And rumors began to circulate.

"Somehow, there's something spooky about her, huh."

"Do you think she's some kind of monster?"

Nevertheless, the woman paid no attention to what was being said and continued on submissively, working very hard.

Life went on like this day by day, but one night a greedy man from the village called secretly on the woman and said,

"I have something to ask of you. There is a sake shop by the side of the highway, and the owner is rich. In his storehouse, there are three jars filled with gold coins. I'd like you to borrow just one of them and bring it here."

Hearing this, the woman replied sharply, "Well, young master, you're saying 'borrow,' but doesn't that amount to stealing?"

"Oh, no," he answered. "I'm going to borrow it. Just borrow it and put it in the house."

"If so, why would you want to put it there?" she asked.

"Well, to use the gold coins. But I will return them in three years for sure."

"Well then, write up a promise to that effect for the sake shop owner."

"I've already talked to him about this, and told him that you're coming tonight. He consented to this and said that you could go inside the storehouse. Look! Here's the key." And he dangled a key in front of her eyes.

With this turn of the conversation, the woman felt relieved and took the key. "Well then, I'll be off," she said, making ready to go.

But the man got scared and said, "Don't tell anyone about this. If other people learn about it, they'll be envious. And don't bring the jar to my house right away but put it in your hut for the time being."

"Understood." When the night deepened, the trusting woman went to the sake shop's storehouse as she was told, shouldered one of the jars containing gold coins and put it in her own hut, as instructed.

Two days later, the voice of the sake-shop owner rang through the village. "Someone has stolen a jar of my gold coins!" he cried, causing a great uproar among the villagers, and all eyes fell upon the woman.

Stomping their way to her hut, the villagers quickly discovered the jar. The woman disclosed that she had done this at the greedy man's request, but no one believed her. They attacked the hut, and suddenly the woman changed into a frightening Yamamba mountain witch.

"Ahh, the world of men!" she said. "Do they think at all? Well, this is goodbye!" and, with those words, she floated up to the top of her hut.

Seeing this, without a moment's delay, a hunter took his

rifle and shot at her. But the Yamamba's body was not hit, and an unexpected voice came from nowhere and announced, "The world of men will not last long. Ahh, how sad, how sad!" Then the Yamamba's ghostly form rose above the clouds and flew off to nobody knew where.

Now, in the era in which we live, the world has come close to the Yamamba's prediction.

The Yamamba's Daughter

One day the daughter of a Yamamba mountain witch said, "Mother, just once I'd like to try going into a human village and living as someone's wife."

"I understand how you feel," the Yamamba replied, trying to detain her daughter. "But you know, in a human village, the people will try to deceive you and, well, it will not be very satisfactory."

"But I want to see what it's like being a wife," the daughter pleaded.

"But with a face like yours, humans will run away, thinking you're a monster," said her mother. "You will never find someone who will be your husband."

And for sure, the Yamamba's daughter looked exactly like her mother—her mouth was split from ear to ear, her eyes turned upwards and she had horns growing out of her head as well.

But the daughter kept pleading, her eyes full of tears, until her mother said, "Well, if you want it that much, go on down to the village and look for a husband. But it will be in vain with that face."

With that, she had her daughter drink some medicine that had been put in a jar and the girl's appearance gradually changed into that of a beautiful young woman.

"Now then, this should be fine," the Yamamba said, and had her daughter look into a mirror.

The daughter was overjoyed, but anxiously asked, "Now, what should I do?"

"There's no problem," the mother replied. "Just go down to the village, stand at the crossroads and sing the weaver's song you know so well."

So before the day was over, the daughter went down to the

village crossroads, and when she sang the weaver's song, a crowd gathered, charmed by her voice.

Then, someone in the crowd came forward and said, "Won't you be my wife?"

And with that, one young man after another approached her, until she stood with a perplexed expression and said, "As for me, the poorest and most foolish in the village . . ." She paused, took a breath, and announced, "The most gullible man would be fine."

Hearing that, there was a general stir among the men in the crowd, but they then fell silent, as no one wanted that label applied to him.

Just then, one man laughed and said, "The only one who would fit that description would be Kamesa."

This quickly occurred to the rest of them and they all turned around. Kamesa was standing drooling open-mouthed in front of a Buddhist statue of Jizo, far from the others.

"Well, to have such a man become this woman's husband would be a real waste."

People began murmuring such things, but despite these words about Kamesa, the Yamamba's daughter went to him the very next day, became his wife and began weaving.

However, after a number of days, Kamesa's mother went in the middle of the night to look in on the room where her son's wife was sleeping, and there the woman was in her true appearance as a Yamamba!

"Oh no! This is horrible!" the shocked woman said to herself and went to inform her son.

But her son simply said, "Oh, is that so?" and did not look the least bit perturbed.

"Listen, you!" his mother said. "She is a Yamamba! Is that all right with you? Think about it. You've been deceived."

"That's all right, isn't it? Being deceived is fine with me," replied Kamesa.

Now the mother and the bride were both hard workers, and after this exchange, the disturbance was over. Not only that, but the cloth woven by the Yamamba's daughter was more beautiful than anyone had seen, and surprised everyone so much that it sold quite well.

Kamesa never disclosed this secret to anyone and, it is said that they lived happily ever after.

The Smelly Priest and the Yamamba

There was a priest whose robes were dirty and who hardly bathed at all and so he was called "the smelly priest."

Well then, while this priest was traveling, he had gone round and about and had finally come to a village at the foot of Mount Mushikura, near the Zenkoji Temple.

At that time a Yamamba mountain witch would sometimes come down to the village. She would get angry and cause terror and distress to the villagers by ravaging the rice fields and even demanding their babies. So when the priest arrived, someone said, "Let's have the priest pray so that the Yamamba will not come any more." But as he was a smelly priest, no one would let him stay at their house.

"We're truly sorry," said one of the villagers, "but if you would go up on Mount Mushikura, there's a cave where you could stay. You'll see two caves, side by side. The entrance to one is wet with thick moss. In the entrance to the other, no moss is growing at all. You should use the one thick with moss."

"Why is that?"

"Well, that one . . . that one has a cool breeze."

"Ahh, that would be a blessing. There is nothing quite so nice when sleeping in a rocky cave."

The truth was that the Yamamba was using the cave where no moss grew, and if the villagers had said this, they thought that the smelly priest would be displeased, so no one spoke of this matter.

Well then, when the priest departed, the bad smell that had been wafting through the village left on the wind, and everyone felt better. Now when the priest entered the cave where the moss grew, as he had been told to, the breeze coming from the depths of the cave gave him such a good feeling that soon he went to sleep, snoring away.

But the sound of his snoring was so noisy that the Ya-mamba, who was sleeping in the cave next door, opened her eyes and yelled, "Who's in there?"

Leaping up, she stuck her head into the other cave. But in an instant—whoof!—a terrible smell completely over-whelmed the Yamamba.

"Ahh! What a stink!" And she fled in complete panic. But the smelly wind chased after her, even as she ran away. In the end, she collided with the main gate of the Zenkoji Temple and died instantly.

After the village people heard of this, it is said that they never again mistreated or avoided smelly people who came around, but treated them kindly.

PART 7

YOKAI AND SHAPE-SHIFTERS, ONE AFTER ANOTHER

The Onbu-Obake Piggyback Ghost

This is a story about the Kiso Road.

On a certain part of the road, where it passed through the mountains, travelers and local villagers would sometimes, at night, hear a strange voice calling "*Obaritee, obaritee.*" ("Carry me, carry me.") It was a sad sort of voice, and everyone was so shocked that they nearly fell over and, throwing away whatever they were carrying, fled for their lives. There were also those who felt a hand grabbing them by the back.

"That's frightening, huh? I won't want to take that road again!" Talk everywhere was that this was not some trivial matter, and if not stopped soon, many lives would be lost.

Another troublesome matter was that the ox drivers who transported food to the village would no longer come at all. Among themselves the ox drivers said that in going to such a place, one might not come back, and that this would hardly make business worthwhile.

🔥 🔥 🔥

One day, a samurai was passing through and laughed, saying, "What? You're frightened by such a thing? I'll take care of this!" and stayed there at the village. He thereupon ate a large dinner and when night came, he swaggered out to the pass with a "Well, I'll take care of this now."

The wind turned cold, the branches of the trees rustled in an unpleasant way and from somewhere he could hear the voice, "*Obaritee, obaritee.*"

"Humph! It's finally here." At hearing the voice, even the samurai was frightened, but remembering that he was a samurai, he pulled himself together and summoned up as much courage as he could.

"Hey! Onbu-obake, piggyback ghost! Come on out!" And just as he yelled this, he felt a hand grabbing at his back. The samurai thought that the ghost had come and, with a shout, swung his sword behind him.

Crying out as though in pain, something that looked like a hedgehog fell to the ground.

"What? A hedgehog?" he laughed. And sheathing his sword, he calmly retreated back to the village and said to the villagers, "Now you can be at peace. It was truly laughable that you thought there was a ghost. It was only a hedgehog. Tomorrow morning you should go take a look." And with that, he knocked back some sake.

However, the next day when the villagers climbed up to the pass to see for themselves, there was no dead body of a hedgehog. The only thing there was a large pine branch.

"What's this? The samurai said that it was without a doubt a hedgehog, but, well, maybe he was bewitched."

When the villagers returned and were talking this over, the samurai, who had woken up after sleeping off the sake he drank said, "What? You're saying it was a branch?" and shocked, left the place hurriedly.

The next person who arrived hoping to vanquish the ghost he had heard stories about was a hunter.

"I'm from the southern regions," he declared, "and I have just come from conquering the huge Daija snake of Hida with this rifle. This Onbu-obake is a small thing—you can leave it to me." With this, he was treated to sake by the villagers and, in high spirits, he spent the evening entertaining them with stories of his past brave exploits.

Meanwhile, the night grew dark.

"It looks like we can have confidence this time," the villagers said together, and saw the hunter off as he walked out into the night.

When the hunter reached the pass, he felt embarrassed by all the lies he had told up until now, and stood stock still. Then, from the midst of the darkness he could hear that voice:

"*Obaritee, obaritee.*"

He was in fact a cowardly hunter, and instantly he felt that his blood was being drained from his body. In fact his fear was such that he was unable to stand. And wasn't that a shining eye approaching him from the midst of the darkness? The hunter triggered his gun again and again as though he was in a trance.

As a black shadow assailed him, he unsheathed his woodsman's hatchet and swung it around in confusion. But whatever it was did not run away. Scuffling like this until dawn, the hunter collapsed, exhausted.

The villagers were worried and climbed up to the pass, where they found that the thicket all around the collapsed hunter had been wildly slashed. Surprised, they held their thoughts in silence and said not a word.

Well then, the next person who passed through the village was a *yamabushi* mountain monk who, when he heard about the Onbu-obake, said, "What kind of talk is this? I have great willpower and I've lost count of the number of ghosts I have defeated just with that."

After being treated generously by the villagers, he waited for night to fall and then set out to climb up the pass. The villagers, who thought for sure that this time the ghost would be defeated, waited in anticipation.

However, this yamabushi was also a coward and felt nervous and uneasy just at the sound of the rustling of the trees. Suddenly, just as the place became quiet, the same sad voice could be heard coming out of the dark.

"*Obaritee, obaritee.*"

The yamabushi was terrified and took out his conch shell, which he blew over and over again, trying to conquer his fear. However, the sound that had surprised him had not been made by the Onbu-obake, but instead by the mountain's birds and beasts. And when they had fled through the forests and thickets, a silence returned.

"Come on out, you Onbu-obake!" he shouted, recovering some of his spirit. "I guess you're afraid to appear. Fine, fine." And with that hasty conclusion, he returned to the village.

"Well, now. I have completely confined the Onbu-obake by the power of my will," he said calmly. "You will not see it again."

Hearing this, the villagers thanked him profusely, and treated him with great respect.

Now, having received a great deal of money from the village headman, he happily went on his way. Nevertheless, the Onbu-obake had not been pacified at all. That very night, "*Obaritee, obaritee*" was heard again, frightening everyone.

The villagers had by this time been deceived by three men, and felt that there was nothing they could do, when one day an old lady who lived deep in the mountains far beyond was traveling down to this village. Her daughter had married into a family in a distant place and had just given birth, and the old lady, overwhelmed with joy at the thought of her first grandchild, was on her way to visit.

Now, just as she approached the pass that led to the village, the night came on completely. And just as she mumbled to herself that this was the place where the Onbu-obake appeared, she heard the voice, saying, "*Obaritee, obaritee.*"

But the old lady could think of nothing but her grandchild and had the illusion that it was the new baby's voice.

"So you want to be carried? Why don't you climb onto this old lady's back," she said without thinking twice. Then, indeed, something had climbed onto her back. It gave her the feeling of a hand grabbing her back, but thinking only of her grandchild, it was not unpleasant.

"Sleep, sleep now,
Listen, sleep, sleep now ..."

And she walked along, singing lullabies. The Onbu-obake was completely surprised at this, but enjoyed the good feeling that the song gave, and as it was carried along it began to quietly snore.

Soon dawn broke and the morning light shone dazzlingly. In the distance ahead of her, the old lady could see the roofs of the village where her daughter had gone as a bride.

At that moment she realized that it would be strange if her grandchild were actually on her back, and that it must be the Onbu-obake for sure. Looking around, what she saw was the cute face of a Tanuki raccoon-dog yokai. The Tanuki awoke and was so surprised when it realized where it actually was that it quickly jumped down to the ground.

The old lady looked at its face intently and said in a loud voice, "Oh, my goodness! Aren't you the little Tanuki whose mother was recently shot by the old man who is my neighbor? Here now, climb back up and I'll carry you on my back some more." And she beckoned it to her. But the little Tanuki, although it looked as though it would like to do just that, looked back once or twice and then disappeared into a thicket.

And from that time, the Onbu-obake never appeared at the pass again.

Or so it is said.

The Long Red Hand That Came Out of the Lake

In the past, there were many stories here and there about Kappa water sprites coming out of a river onto land and pulling horses in to drown. But this is a strange story about the time a horse driver was passing by a pond, when a red hand emerged from the water, grabbed the horse by the tail and dragged the entire animal under the surface.

And this story has much to do with a heartless lord.

In a certain village, a pretty little girl called O-setsu was born into the house of the village headman. As she grew up, the villagers would often say, "O-setsu will be watched and loved by the men of this place, but as for her, who will she pick?" and looked forward to seeing what would happen.

However, when O-setsu grew up to be a beautiful young lady, the one her heart was drawn to most was Zentaro, who worked for the village headman. The two of them would slip away from the house at night and talk lovingly together. The place where they always met was at the edge of a pond surrounded by zelkova trees at a little distance from the house.

"O-setsu," the young man said, "I have watched you from the time you were small and it was my intention to know you more than other men. I remember the day you were born, when swallows and doves flocked to your side to sing their welcome to this beautiful new baby." Talking to her like this, mixing together things that had happened and things that hadn't happened, he stole her affection and made her happy.

Drawn to the gentle Zentaro, O-setsu, from her side, waited for him to ask her to be his bride.

But one day when O-setsu was walking by the edge of the pond, she heard someone shouting at her from behind.

Turning to look, it was the local lord mounted on a horse, accompanied by a number of retainers, one of whom cautioned her to listen to what would be said. Without dismounting, the lord asked,

"You're a pretty girl. What's your name?"

"Well, my name is Setsu."

"Aha. All right, O-setsu," he said, using the polite form of her name. "Where do you live?"

"Well . . . ," she mumbled, looking down.

At this, a retainer informed the lord that she was the daughter of the village headman. At which, the lord said, "O-setsu, huh. I'll put you to some kind of work. I'll send you a nice note." And he whipped his horse and departed.

O-setsu felt that this was somehow a bad omen, and a month passed. One day a retainer came from the castle and stepped up into the headman's house.

"Could we talk about O-setsu being employed by the lord, please?" said the retainer.

The headman was shocked and replied ambiguously, "This is very generous, but . . ."

"This is an order from the lord," the retainer said roughly, and went outside. O-setsu, who had fled the village, was now caught near the aforementioned pond and lifted onto a horse. Just then, Zentaro dashed up.

"Honorable samurai, please listen!" and tried to hold the retainer back.

"What impudence! This important woman is going to serve at the castle. A lowly man like you cannot touch her with a single finger," and he galloped along the side of the pond and tried to leave.

"Wait!" shouted Zentaro, his frantic voice echoing all around. "Please wait!"

Suddenly the samurai unsheathed his sword and cut off Zentaro's hand, which was grasping the horse's tail. Zentaro tumbled, then fell, blood-stained, and sank into the pond.

After that, if anyone passed by the pond, a long red hand would rise from the water.

The Haunted House

Long ago, there were many stories about the appearance of ghosts, but there was an outlandishly peculiar person living in a particular house, and this strange story is about that.

A certain man came from the countryside to a village, found a house and was delighted when told by the landlord, "I won't need any rent."

Thinking this was a bit strange, the man walked around the neighborhood, asking questions in a casual manner.

"You know there's a ghost in the house you're moving into?" someone said. "It might be hard to deal with, but it may amount to nothing at all."

"If there really is a ghost, I'd like to meet it," the man replied. "Well then, good luck," the neighbor returned.

The man now realized the reason why his house was rent free, but was intrigued by the possibility of encountering a ghost. One night, soon after he had moved into the house, it struck him that he still hadn't encountered the ghost, but just as he was snuggling down under his futon he saw it—a little Hitotsume Kozo one-eyed goblin, standing by his pillow.

"Ahh, welcome, welcome," said the man. "I worked too hard moving in and threw out my shoulder. Would you kindly rub my shoulder?"

"What?" the Hitotsume Kozo exclaimed. "Aren't you frightened?" But as it spoke, it began to rub the man's shoulder.

When this was done, the man continued, "Don't go yet. I went to bed without eating dinner. There's some mochi rice cake over there, so please warm it up." And he pointed to a small kitchen range and the mochi off to the side.

The little Hitotsume Kozo worked away as instructed and the man thought that it was quite cute.

"Goodness. You're a strange ghost," he said, and the two of

them ate the mochi together. Then the man continued, "Ahh, that's right. There's one other request I'd like to make. I just moved in, and the room is rather dirty. I'm sorry to ask, but could you take a rag and wipe it down?"

"Certainly," the Hitotsume Kozo replied, got immediately to work, and then made to go home.

"Oh, I remembered one more thing," said the man. "Could you fill up the water jar and bucket? I'd be in trouble if there were a fire." Saying this, he had the Hitotsume Kozo fill the containers up with water. And then, "Well, that's fine. Thanks for all your help."

"Good-bye," said the Hitotsume Kozo and went away. Truly, it was a strange ghost.

The next night a huge three-eyed Onyudo yokai in the form of a giant monk, appeared. It was so big that it was barely able to enter the house, so the man said, "Ah yes, just right. There are spider nests in the ceiling, and they're all over, can't you see? So would you please clear them away and then wipe down the ceiling with a rag?"

The huge Onyudo did as it was told without complaint.

"Just tonight, there is a full moon. You could weed out the vegetation growing on the thatch," the man continued, "and when you finish with that, trim the tree branches in the garden that are making it so dark."

In this manner, the man managed to put the Onyudo to work for him. Now the night after the Onyudo left, he was at the point of going happily to sleep, thinking that he could deal with any sort of ghost that appeared, when a little Tanuki raccoon-dog yokai ambled in.

"Huh! A Tanuki. What do you know? What was that about the Hitotsume Kozo and the Onyudo?"

"Those were just shapes I took," the Tanuki said, seeming full of regret. "But I've never encountered a man who could tame ghosts like this before."

O-mantaro in the Bottle

O-mantaro had ears like a horse. He was a big man who nearly reached the sky, so he could look down from above the clouds. From his viewpoint on high he could help the locals by telling them things such as the best place to build a dike to prevent a flood and he would even build that dike with his own hands. He was truly a kindhearted man, but the only problem was that, once he drank sake, he would do bad things—so was he good or was he bad?

When he started drinking sake, he would destroy houses and ruin vegetable fields just for fun.

"At this point it would be better to get rid of him," the local people said.

Rumor had it that his evil deeds were caused by the rejection of a beautiful woman who lived in a faraway village.

"First, we must prevent his rampages by prohibiting sake everywhere—even the scent of it."

This injunction was followed, but this still had no result, so the local people declared, "In this case, we will have to subdue him altogether."

One might speak of "subduing," but there was no one with that sort of strength. As the villages spoke together like this, someone said, "I've got it! What about Yotaro?"

"Yotaro, huh?" was the hesitant response. Anyway, when it came to Yotaro, although his body was very big, all he did was sleep.

"But in a contest with O-mantaro, he would win."

"Never!"

"No, no. With his unnatural strength, I've seen him treat a huge rock like it was a handful of sand."

And so it was decided that it would be well to have the two men compete, and several prominent men of the village went to make a request at the hut where Yotaro lived on the outskirts of town.

"Yes, alright," Yotaro said, "I will not be able to subdue him, but I can make him more gentle."

"Ahh, good! But how long will it take?" the men asked.

"Well, one day, I guess," said Yotaro.

"What? That's great! But what will you want as a reward?"

"I would like to take the village headman's daughter, O-hana, as my wife."

The villagers were surprised, but when they returned to the headman and reported this to him, he just said, "Well, there's no way Yotaro could accomplish such a thing, so there's nothing to worry about."

That night, just about midnight, there was a huge clap of thunder, sounding like huge trees crashing to the ground, and everyone jumped up awake. Because the rain was falling in torrents, no one went outside.

At last, the storm abated and when morning came, Yotaro arrived at the headman's house and said "Now then, I've subdued O-mantaro and brought him along." And he held out a small bottle containing O-mantaro. "Now I'll take O-hana as my wife."

The villagers all wore worried expressions. The headman appeared resigned, called in O-hana and explained the circumstances. But O-hana was completely charmed by O-mantaro, now completely shrunk inside the bottle with his knees up and said, "I'll take good care of O-mantaro," and went off to Yotaro's place and became his bride.

A later rumor had it that Yotaro was actually a heaven-sent child.

The Amanojaku Demon and the Melon-Child Princess

In a certain place there lived an old man and an old woman.

The old man would gather firewood in the mountain and the old lady would go to the river to wash clothes. One day, when the old lady was working at the river, a large tiered box came floating down on the current.

When the old lady opened up the box and looked in, she discovered a melon. "Well, well," she said to herself, "This is a curious melon." She put the melon in the cupboard and waited for the old man to come home.

When the old man returned, she told him her story and went to take the melon out of the cupboard. But when she opened the cupboard doors, the melon was not there and in its place a cute little girl was sitting quietly.

"Oh, my! This is a surprise! The melon has turned into a little girl!"

"What do you think?" the old man asked. "Let's name her the Melon-Child Princess."

"Yes, that's a good name," the old lady said happily.

The little girl was so cute that the old couple took great care in bringing her up just as she was.

◊ ◊ ◊

As the Melon-Child Princess grew up, she became very good at weaving, and every day the pleasant sound of the loom echoed through the house. But then one day, when it knew that the old man and the old lady were not at home, an Amanojaku demon came down from the mountain.

"Melon-Child, Melon-Child . . . come here for a moment,"

it said, and took her out next to a pear tree. "Would you dress me just for a moment in your beautiful robe?" And he quickly took off his own filthy clothes and put on the princess's robe. Not only that, but he tied her to the pear tree and went off.

Just as the Melon-Child Princess started to cry, the old man came home. Hearing her story, the old man went out the next day, found the Amanojaku, killed it and threw it out into the pampas grass field. From that day on, the roots of the pampas grass were stained red.

Or so it is said.

The Face-Stroking Ghost

Long ago, there were said to be ghosts who would stroke people's buttocks as they passed by, but this is a story about a ghost called "the Face-Stroker." The Face-Stroker came out at night, but often appeared on a mountain road on dark moonless nights.

Now one night, two carpenter's apprentices, Tsurukichi and Kamekichi, were returning home from a celebration in the neighboring village, when halfway there and drunk, one of them exclaimed, "My feet really hurt and I can't go on. Let's go rest awhile under that cherry tree." And with this, they rested sitting on a rock in the front garden of a temple.

Looking up, Tsurukichi belched forth with sake-stinking breath, "My, how beautiful the cherry blossoms are at night. But then, "Hey! What's this?" he said angrily to Kamekichi, "Why are you stroking my face?"

But now, Kamekichi shouted, "Hey! Hey! You stop it! Why did *you* just stroke *my* face?"

"You're talking foolishness. Would I do such a thing?"

"Well then, who?"

When they knew that they had both been mistaken, they fell silent. "You know, the hand that stroked me was cold."

"Me, too! It was a cold hand."

When their conversation had gotten this far, they began to shudder. "It was the Face-Stroker! The Face-Stroker!" they cried out.

Making a great racket, they ran home as fast as they could. There had been many stories at that time about the face-stroking ghost. It was said that people who had had their faces stroked would come down with a fever and fall right asleep, and of course, these two developed fevers that very night. Talk of the Face-Stroker spread through the village.

"With things like this, even if you have some business and want to go to the next village, it's better not to go at all."

"Even for work."

Everyone continued to feel this sort of anxiety, until . . .

"Look, we'll be fine if we walk along making sure our faces cannot be touched," someone said. And so, wrapping a hand towel over their heads, gradually more and more people went out on the road at night. The Face-Stroker, however, was not just in one village, but in all the villages in the area and the demand for hand towels was very high.

The seller of hand towels went from village to village every day and made a fine profit. And this was much talked about.

"This is strange, huh."

"Where did that hand towel merchant come from?"

With such questions circulating about, it was eventually understood that he came from a faraway village.

Finally, two men went secretly to the towel seller's house. Peeking through a crack in the door, they spied the towel seller and a Hitotsume Kozo one-eyed goblin in a lamplit room talking quietly and laughing together. And around them was a mountain of hand towels.

"So that's it! That's it!"

"We'll teach them a lesson!"

The two hurried home that night and, waiting for the sun to come up, together told everyone their story. With that, the villagers took stones and sickles and, hurrying to the towel seller's house, quickly got a hold of him and handed him over to the magistrate.

As for the Hitotsume Kozo, it is said that a priest from the village went around its house placing amulets, until a little slug came creeping out through the dirt floor and wrote on the ground, "I'm sorry, I'm sorry," in silver letters.

The Azukitogi Yokai

A long time ago, there were Azukitogi yokai here and there, known for making a mysterious noise that sounds like beans being washed. You know that rice is washed clean in a kitchen sink, and you know the sound of it going *shoki shoki*. There are also people who hear the sound of beans being washed as the same sound.

Long ago, when night fell, one could often hear that sound coming from nowhere in particular, and children playing outside would stop what they were doing and go home. At such times, the grown-ups would say, "Look, it must be the Azukitogi here at this late hour," and order the children to stay inside. But no one ever saw the Azukitogi. Nevertheless, walking over a dark bridge or taking a road that few people used, the frightening sound of *shoki shoki* could be heard from somewhere. And when children suddenly could not be found, it was said that they had been taken off by the Azukitogi. The Azukitogi was also heard to sing a scary song:

> Washing beans, *yashoka*
> taking people and eating them,
> *yashoka*
> *shoki shoki shoki*

Now once, a number of young men were going over a bridge crossing a river near the Daimon Pass, when they heard a woman's voice singing that song piteously. Taking cover by hiding next to the bridge, the men looked carefully around them. Then, when they heard the song starting up again, they leapt out with a "Now!" But they could not see her anywhere.

Nowadays, the ghost is no longer around, but what kind of ghost could it have been?

The Yurei That Took Care of a Child

There was once a woman who, while a child was still within her, became sick and died, and was buried in the village. The villagers all felt sorry for her.

Well then, there was a shop in the village, and late every night a woman would come asking to buy candy. The shop keeper thought this was strange and, looking at the money the woman gave him, saw that it was nothing but the leaves of trees. Moreover, the woman's face was similar to the one who had died, so he went to the house of the people who had conducted the funeral and told them his story.

The people of the house responded that it was a bunch of foolishness but became uneasy. Going to the graveyard and digging in the place where the coffin had been buried, they found a baby crying and holding some candy.

"Ahh," they exclaimed among themselves in sorrow, "the dead mother gave birth to a child, but even when she died and became a yurei spirit, she took care of it. A mother's love is a marvelous thing!"

The Clog Ghost and the Boot Ghost

In a certain place, an old lady lived by herself. Every night it was her practice to work on a spinning wheel. Then one night she heard something that sounded like the song of a ghost:

> To do night work alone must be lonely,
> *Karakurin karakurin.*

"How strange," she said, but continued at her work. The following night, she heard the song again:

> To do night work alone must be lonely,
> *Basakurin, basakurin.*

As this continued for a few nights, the woman asked a local young man to come and see what kind of ghost it was. That night, he brought a hatchet and sickle, and waited, hiding in the entrance. Soon, sure enough, the song was heard:

> A woman being alone must be lonely,
> *Karakurin Karakurin.*

"Got you!" the young man yelled, leaping out. But what was this? The ghost was a pair of clogs, dancing on the floor! The young man laughed. The next night he waited again. And sure enough:

> To do night work alone must be lonely,
> *Basakurin basakurin.*

The young man yelled, "Who is it?" But when he looked, well, it was just a pair of straw boots, shuffling across the floor.

The Fireball as Big as a Bath Bucket

This happened the year before Japan was defeated in the Pacific War. In the village of Zenkojidaira, a night meeting had just concluded and people were going home when a number of them looked at the sky and shouted, "Oh! What's that?" A fireball as big as a bath bucket was hovering over the roof of a house and seemed about to descend.

"This must be something of a bad omen," everyone whispered together, and hurried to their homes.

The next day, the sad news arrived that the son of the house over which the fireball had been seen had died in the war. Everyone talked together and concluded that the young man had badly wanted to return home and had died with that yearning, in tears.

PART 8

STRANGE TREES AND FLOWERS

Love's Husband-and-Wife Trees

Long ago, the relationship between landowners and those who worked the land was rather strict, and that was also the case when it came to marriage between these two classes.

Well then, at the foot of Mount Ontake, and separated by a large river, there lived a young man and a beautiful young lady who were in love. The young man, Taizo, was born and raised in the house of a tenant farmer; while the young lady on the other side of the river, O-taki by name, was the daughter of a landowner. The two would avoid people's eyes and spend every day talking together of their love. Despite this, very soon, the people around them noticed what was going on and naturally their parents came to hear of it. Taizo's father scolded him.

"No matter how much you and the landowner's daughter are in love, this is scandalous. Do you think that the landowner would even consider marrying his daughter into this poor house? This is foolish talk."

And his mother also tried to dissuade him. "My real thoughts are, well, I'd like to go along with your feelings," she said. "But her father is a landowner and we're so poor ... Even if she was kind enough to come here, I can see that she would just hang her head in embarrassment."

"But, Mother . . . ," said Taizo, but no words would come out. He knew that even if he spoke, his parents would not listen to him. Compared to the other young men around him, Taizo was easygoing and gentle. Whether at home or at work, he never caused anyone to worry. And perhaps it was his gentle character that attracted O-taki.

In O-taki's home, her father was angry too. "Going to be a bride in such a poor farmer's house would be outrageous and would become nothing more than a joke," he said. And he brought up the story of the daughter of the headman of a neighboring village running off with a poor farmer a few years before. "And you know, it was said that that was because the headman was a man of loose morals."

Continuing this theme, her mother chimed in. "O-taki, if you think that it's all right to smear mud on your mother and father's faces, then you should go and become his wife, but you must never cross this threshold again."

Because the parents of both houses were like this, Taizo and O-taki became very sad, but at night sneaked out into the forest at the Jizo Pass and confirmed their love.

"If it's come to this," O-taki said, "please steal me away."

Recently, her father had brought up a story of an elopement when a headman's daughter had been stolen away by her lover and the two had set out on a journey. They had been guided on this journey by an elder who understood matters of love. O-taki repeated this story in an offhand way and happily rested her head on Taizo's chest.

"Steal you away? Ahh . . ."

Taizo did not have the courage to go that far and could only sigh deeply in despair.

"Please, please," O-taki cried, shedding huge tears.

"I just can't do such a thing," Taizo replied; and the conversation always stopped there.

"If I stole her away and left my home, my father and mother would forsake me as well. That would be awful . . ." Late at night when Taizo returned home, he was unable to sleep, troubled by his inability to find a solution to this problem. "Ahh, should I just give it all up?"

Every night, Taizo would stare at the ceiling, tears flooding his eyes, until the morning light. And O-taki, too, passed her days downcast in the same way.

Summer passed and autumn came to an end. Their parents kept a sharp watch on them and they were unable to meet. One night, when the first snow of the winter had started to fall and flutter about, O-taki's mother said, "Are you still thinking about Taizo?" Then, unexpectedly she added, "You

should not carry it too far. You should wait to receive a better proposal."

O-taki heard this and turned pale.

"You don't have to worry about it. Your father is thinking this over carefully," she continued, then said no more.

Hearing this, O-taki could not suppress her feelings and went to where her father was sleeping. "Why didn't you talk to me about this?" she demanded vehemently. "I'm not going to get married to anyone."

In fact, her father had begun to settle a marriage proposal with the son of a landowner one village away.

"Now, now. Calm down," he said. And then told her that he had arranged a felicitous marriage for her in the spring. "If you marry this landowner's son and go to his house, the place has a garden more than twice the size of ours and there are seven storehouses."

That night O-taki cried and cried until dawn.

Then, three days later in the afternoon, the two, whose love had grown stronger and stronger, slipped out of their homes and sat down on a fallen tree in the forest at the Jizo Pass. And there they stayed embracing each other.

"I wanted be with you!"

"Me, too. With you."

The hands that held each other gradually warmed and the snow that had begun to fall melted over the back of those hands. As Taizo listened to the story of O-taki's wedding proposal, he grew sad.

"We may never be able to meet again," he said tearfully.

"No, no. Because I'm not doing it."

"Really?"

"Yes."

As they exchanged these words, the snow fell harder and harder and gradually enveloped the two of them.

"Together . . . forever . . ."

"Yes . . ."

Eventually, Mount Ontake and all the villages beyond it disappeared in the billowy flakes of snow, and soon, night fell. But the couple did not leave the pass, but spent the night there calmly.

The villagers remarked to each other how cold it was and how such a large snowfall was a rare event, but the two lovers, consumed with joy, did not notice the cold. Even as night came, they held each other and, as if in a dream, their consciousness dimmed. Eventually, the snow completely covered them, and when it began to abate a little, the beautiful stars in the sky shone as if to bless them.

During the night, there were great commotions in the houses of both Taizo and O-taki, but even with the dawn and for days after, the two could not be found.

Before long, winter passed, spring arrived and new buds bloomed on the trees. And those who walked over the pass discovered two maple trees they had not seen before. The branches of the two trees were intertwined as though drawing close to each other and reached into the sky. Even more strangely, Taizo and O-taki's clothes were beneath the trees.

The villagers for the first time realized that these were the figures of the two lovers and offered solemn prayers to them. And from that time on, they called them "Love's Husband-and-Wife Trees."

After that, the custom began that a man and woman in love who thought that their parents would not agree to their union, would go to the trees, tear off a bit of the sleeves of their undergarments, tie them to the trees and pray that they could be together.

This story was conveyed far and wide, and eventually these pieces of cloth covered the branches of these trees. When the cloth fluttered in the wind, the trees became a beautiful sight.

Or so it is said.

The Seeds of the Pepper Tree from the Ryugu Palace

Many years ago, some Japanese pepper tree seeds were delivered to a temple in northern Shinano from the Ryugu Palace deep below the Northern Sea, the home of Ryu-O, the Dragon King. A surprising event.

The one who carried the seeds to Shinano was a child of the Ryugu Palace. One day this child was playing in the palace garden on the seabed, picking up the seeds of the pepper tree that was growing there, when he was told by Ryu-O to take a box to the Zen'oji Temple.

"What's inside?" the child asked as a brilliant gold box was put before him.

"That's a secret," Ryu-O replied, tightly tying a cord around the box. "The moment I speak of it, it will instantly disappear. And you must not open it on your way," he warned the child.

"Well then, why is this going to the Zen'oji Temple?" the child continued to inquire.

"Yes, well you've asked a good question," came the reply. "It's because the priests at the temple and the villagers are honest and good-natured people. All right, then. Off you go."

Given this explanation, with a sweet look on his face, the child shouldered the box and went up, up, up from the bottom of the sea. He then went along a river and, after getting lost once or twice, found his way to the Kanman Waterfall deep in the Kutsuno area of northern Shinano.

The child ascended the waterfall and, aching from his long journey, sat on top of a large rock to catch his breath while he gazed intently at the golden box he had shouldered. The more he looked at it, being a young child, the more he was tempted to look inside.

If he delivered the box to the temple, he would not be able to look inside himself, he realized. His curiosity grew and grew and finally he was unable to resist. He untied the cord and opened the lid of the box. Immediately, a thunderous sound that shook heaven and earth rang out and before he knew it, some extraordinarily large thing rolled into the basin of the waterfall.

The child was so shocked that he lost consciousness and lay collapsed there for a while. Then, when he at last opened his eyes, he was aware that the box had disappeared. "Now I've done it!" he thought. This was terrible and if he went home now, he would receive a royal punishment from Ryu-O. But when he looked around, he found that the golden box was behind him.

"Ahh!" The child heaved a sigh of relief, picked up the box and checked inside it. But it was empty. Was it that large thing that had rolled out? In his grief at having lost something important, the child was at a loss of what to do and hung his head.

"If I return, I'll be punished . . ."

Just then, some things fell out of his breast pocket and when he picked them up and looked carefully, they were two seeds of the Japanese pepper tree. Having no other recourse, the child put the seeds into the box, fastened the lid, tightly tied the cord around it and thought, "This is better than there being nothing inside at all."

Finally, the child took in a deep breath and, asking directions from the villagers one after another, arrived at the Zen'oji Temple. He then met the priest and informed him that he had come from the Ryugu Palace.

"Well now," the priest said, looking at the child as though quite impressed, "I'm surprised that you've come from the faraway Ryugu Palace, as you are yet quite small. So, what is your mission?"

With this being asked of him, the child breathed a sigh of relief as he understood that the priest had heard nothing from Ryu-O.

"Well, actually . . ." Explaining why Ryu-O had sent him, he presented the box.

The priest smiled, seemingly embarrassed and said, "Goodness, what a splendid box. But what good deeds have I done to deserve such praise? What welcome kindness. When you return, please express my deep gratitude to Ryu-O. And thank you for all your trouble."

And thus, he saw him off at the gate.

Well then, after that, the priest loosened the cord, opened the box and looked inside. But there was nothing but two seeds from a tree.

"Huh?" For a second, he cocked his head to one side and thought for sure that there must have been a reason why Ryu-O had a messenger like that purposefully bring this along. "Well then, since they are the seeds of a tree, he must want me to plant them," he mumbled and the very next day he planted them on the premises.

Before the year was out, the seeds began to sprout and grow quickly. One of the trees only produced flowers, while the other was heavy with berries.

"Ah ha! These are strange trees," he thought. "Just the kind of pepper trees you might expect from the Ryugu Palace."

After that, the priest had the villagers bring their children to the temple, and as presents they all happily received seeds to plant in their own gardens. And planting the seeds came to be associated with bringing happiness. In fact, the relationships of married couples that were fighting would improve, and lost children would come home.

As for the pepper trees that only bore flowers, they grew not only in the temple grounds, but throughout the village and sent out a wonderful aroma.

◊　　◊　　◊

One day, the priest was dozing off when he heard a solemn voice: "The real gift of the young messenger was a bell, which is now sunk in the Kanman waterfall. I sent it because the

Zen'oji Temple has no bell." With this message from Ryu-O, the priest immediately went to the waterfall to take a look. And sure enough, sunk deep in the water was a large temple bell. It was so heavy that even all of the villagers together, though they pulled and pulled, were unable to raise it from the bottom.

Not long after that, the priest was dozing off again when he heard the voice say, "If you are unable to bring it up, there's nothing to be done. Instead, I will ring it for you at night."

And just as Ryu-O had said, the beautiful sound of the bell coming from the bottom of the waterfall could be heard in every corner of the village. And when they heard that sound, it was as though the entire village had the feeling of being filled with the atmosphere of the Buddhist Pure Land paradise.

Well then, what about after the child messenger to the Ryugu Palace? As Ryu-O was very broad-minded, he just laughed and laughed upon the child's return, and praised him for having been able to make such a journey to such a faraway place alone, even though so young.

The Princess and the Nutmeg Tree

It seems that somehow the hearts of human beings and trees are connected.

Long ago, a princess was born in the mansion of the lord of Nezu. As time went on, she grew up, and one autumn day when she had reached the age of seven, the princess went out to the mountain behind the mansion, where she saw a tree laden with shining golden-colored seeds. And her heart was completely taken by that tree.

The tree was a nutmeg, and when she walked beneath it, she was astonished at the sight of all the seeds that had fallen to the ground.

"My, how beautiful!" she exclaimed, and picked up one of them. As she looked at the seed in the palm of her hand, she seemed to hear a voice saying, "I am happy to be gathered up by the princess..."

The princess was so pleased that she began picking up the seeds one after another and putting them into the sleeve of her red kimono. She then ran back to the mansion happily, telling everyone to look at what she had found, laughing and showing her white teeth.

"Really! Such pretty seeds!" her wet nurse said and, teaching her the name of the tree, showed her how she could play with the seeds. Taking a needle, she opened a hole in each seed, strung a thread through the holes, made a necklace and put it around the princess's neck. The princess exclaimed that she wanted to try that herself. Taking the needle and thread from the wet nurse, she opened holes in the seeds she gathered, one after another, passed the thread through them and made a great number of necklaces. Pleased with her accomplishment, she ran throughout the mansion putting the necklaces around everybody's necks.

So, thanks to the princess, the hearts of the bored master and all of his retainers were diverted and amused.

◊   ◊   ◊

From that time on, every year with the coming of autumn, the princess would go out to the mountain behind the mansion and enjoy gathering the seeds of the nutmeg tree. And in this way, the princess went through her childhood years.

Well then, while the princess continued making her necklaces, she happened to drop just one of the seeds to the ground, and it sprouted. Eventually, as the princess became one year and then two years older, the sprout grew and became a large tree. Then, when the princess left the mansion to become a bride, the tree had quite grown in height, its limbs had spread and it was full of golden, shining seeds.

As the princess grew older, her eyes dimmed and she would look in the direction of the mansion from the place where she now lived, and she seemed to be able to see the tree that had grown so luxuriantly large.

Strangely enough, when children came to gather the seeds of that tree, they found that there were holes in them. And it was true, the tree had not forgotten how loved it had been by the princess.

From then on, even after the princess had passed away, the seeds that fell from the huge tree that now seemed to reach the sky, always had open holes in them. The villagers carried those seeds back home with them and, as they cooked them over the fire, talked about the princess and marveled at how delicious the seeds were.

The Ginkgo Tree of Yoshida

In the Chinju Forest near the village of Yoshida, was a marvelous large ginkgo tree. Because it was so striking, travelers would come by to gaze at it and, it was said, were never disappointed. In the summers, it would become luxuriantly green and in the fall its yellow leaves would glitter beautifully as they were blown by the wind. Ginkgo nuts would fall plentifully beneath it, and people would gather them up so that they could roast them.

"What a blessing," they would say. "I've never tasted anything this savory." And they spent their days in anticipation, waiting for the nuts to fall.

Well then, one evening, when the first snow of the season was about to fall in the village, a lone priest arrived from the east. It had been a cold day and, in anticipation of the snowfall, people closed up their doors early.

The priest clutched his torn robes that were fluttering in the wind and, wondering where he might stay the night, stood looking around for a house in the vicinity. His eyes came to rest on a place surrounded by a high wall and he went through the gate. The grounds were rather expansive and full of planted shrubbery. Surely this must be the house of the village headman.

"Excuse me," the priest called at the entrance, and footsteps could be heard coming down a long corridor.

"What do you want?" the woman of the house asked, looking suspiciously at the shabbily dressed priest.

"Well, I'm truly sorry to turn up unexpectedly, but I'm a traveler and I wonder if I might stay here for one night."

The woman stood there and replied in a sympathetic way, "Well, well, how pitiful to have no place to stay in this bad weather." But then she added coldly, "The master is not here today and I cannot put someone up without consulting him."

But just then, the sound of someone clearing his throat could be heard from inside.

"Aha!" the priest thought and, hanging his head and looking toward the gate, replied, "That's certainly reasonable. Sorry to trouble you." Then, standing there and looking up to the sky, remarked, "The ginkgo tree in the Chinju Forest is calm and serene tonight, and snow is coming. That alone would be fine, but the fate of that person is something to regret." And, reciting the Nembutsu Buddhist chant, departed.

Witnessing this, the woman grumbled, "What kind of nonsense was that dirty old priest talking about?" and disappeared behind the door.

Circling the mansion wall, the priest mumbled to himself, "The bigger his mansion, the harder his heart."

Next, the priest spied a small crooked hut, which didn't even have a gate. "Excuse me," he called, standing at the door. As there was no response, he opened the wooden door and called out once again. A man sitting cross-legged at the hearth looked up at him in surprise. Recognizing that his visitor was a priest, he hastily approached him and sat down in a proper way.

"What is it?" the man asked, looking up.

"The fact is, I'm on a journey," the priest replied, and then asked if he might stay the night.

"Ahh, honored priest," the man then said. "In such a dirty place as this . . ." Looking over at his wife, who was cuddling a baby in the corner, he pulled her toward him and said "Give him some welcoming words . . ."

"The baby is crying, and it's too much to ask to have you sleep on some matting, but if that is all right with you . . . ," she answered.

"Well, I was just thinking that I would have to sleep under a tree to have kept off tonight's snow." The priest then put his palms together in thanks and availed himself of the couple's kindness.

The man said, "We have nothing to offer you, but I can at

least let you sit by the hearth. Please, this way." And, breaking up some branches, he added them to the fire that was burning there.

The priest then held his frozen hands to the fire and thanked the two for their graciousness.

After a short while, the man's wife, who had withdrawn into the interior, came out and offered the priest a bowl of steaming soup, saying, "I'm sorry, this is all we have."

"No, no," the priest rejoined. "It was impolite of me to become a sudden guest. This is truly such a blessing!" and happily sipped the soup.

That night, the priest wrapped himself up on a straw mattress in a back room and fell asleep, but was awakened by the baby's crying in the middle of the night. The cries went on and on with no promise of ending, so he went out to the hearth next to the wife who was cuddling the baby. The woman then apologized in shame.

"No, no," the priest said. "There is no need to apologize. Rather than that, tell me what the matter is."

"My breasts will not produce milk, no matter how much I try," she said, truly distressed. "The reason the baby is crying, poor thing, is because I have no milk to give him."

Hearing this, the priest thought for a moment, then said slowly, "There is a wonderful ginkgo tree in this village. Peel off just a little of the bark and boil it. Then drink it."

And with this strange announcement, he returned to the room where he had been sleeping.

The wife and her husband greeted the next day half in doubt, but the priest did not get up at all, and when they went to look in at him, he was nowhere to be seen. All he had left was a narrow paper tablet on which was written the Buddhist holy chant, Namu Amida Butsu.

"Ahh, the priest left early for some reason, and didn't want to wake us."

"What kind of priest was he?"

The two shook their heads in wonder, but then the baby started to cry again.

"Listen," the woman said to her husband. "Could you please go over to the Chinju Forest and peel off a little bark from the ginkgo tree?"

The man went quickly to do this, then boiled the tree bark and gave it to his wife to drink. And in just moments . . .

"Oh, my! It's coming out, it's coming out!"

When the woman pinched her nipple just a little, her milk appeared to splash out. She put her nipple in the baby's mouth and he greedily gulped the delicious liquid down.

"Honored priest. Thank you!"

"That priest was not just an ordinary monk."

The two talked together, and kept the paper tablet the priest had left as a holy treasure.

On the other hand, as the snow piled up in her garden, the woman from the big house with the high wall who had turned him away suddenly recalled what the priest had murmured the night before: "The ginkgo in the Chinju Forest is calm . . ."

Her heart racing, she went out to the forest to take a look, and sure enough, all the ginkgo tree's leaves had fallen to the ground, even though they had been so luxuriant until that day . . . And she then started to feel anxious, remembering the other words he had said: "The fate of that person is something to regret. Ahh, Namu Amida Butsu. Namu Amida Butsu."

Who was "that person"?

She quickly understood that it was herself and began to shudder uncontrollably. And that night she came down with a fever, could not wake up, and expired within seven days.

For a long time after that, the Yoshida ginkgo tree was spoken of as an aid to mothers who could not produce milk. The priest who had taught them about this and then moved on was said to have perhaps been the Buddhist saint, Kobo Daishi. But was this really so? No one knows if it wasn't perhaps another priest, after all. There are in this wide world many kind and gentle-hearted priests.

PART 9

UNENDING MIRACLES OF THE GODS AND BUDDHAS

The Man Who Saw the God

Though you go to the shrine to pray, you will not see the god of that shrine. It is unnecessary to see him, but to want to see him is human nature.

Well then, in the town of Suwa, there was a man of deep faith. He went every day to pray to the god of Suwa, but after a thousand days, he could finally endure it no more.

"Honored God," he began. And, facing the hall of worship of the shrine, he put his hands together in prayer and continued, "Thank you for always looking over us. It is my desire to express my gratitude before your visible form, but I have been unable to actually see you. If you please, could you appear to me just one time in your visible form . . ."

Then a grave voice resounded from within the shrine, "Your deep faith is laudable, but it is impossible to see my true form, for I am something like the wind."

"That . . . that is more than I can bear," the man sighed.

"Well then, if that is so," the god replied, "I'll create a method to be visible just once. But it will not be my true form. If I were to appear in another form, then it would have to be in the form of a human being."

"Huh?"

"Yes. And that human being will be an innocent little boy. If I take on the form of such a child, then your wish will be fulfilled."

"Well, how should I find the child?"

"That will depend on your effort. You should search for the child yourself. If you should see a deer with a split ear . . ."

And with this, the voice disappeared into silence.

"Honored God! Honored God!" But no matter how the man pleaded, there was no further response.

After that, the man began to search for a child that would

fit the description the god had given. Nevertheless, as he was looking only for a young boy, there was no reason that the child might be found; and after a number of years passed, even this man of such deep faith forgot about it all.

◊   ◊   ◊

One day, the man went out hunting. Going deeper and deeper into the forest, he eventually became lost. Standing confused at a place where the path divided into two, he thought he heard the sound of hooves coming from behind, and sure enough, three horses appeared in single file, loaded with various bundles of straw. The horses continued on in front of the man, but there was no one holding them by the reins.

"Now this is strange!" the man thought, cocking his head to one side. Wondering where they were going and what kind of person was waiting for them, he thought that he would like to purchase such clever animals. Then he wondered if someone was actually living this deep in the forest.

The man followed along behind the horse, thinking all the while how mysterious this was. Just then, the horses came to a stop before the entrance to a cave that opened into a cliff and the leading horse began to whinny. With that, a single deer leapt out of the cave.

Looking carefully, the man saw that the deer's ear was split lengthwise. Surely, this was the deer of which the god had spoken. Thinking that he now might be able to encounter the god, the man watched the horses and the deer from a distance.

Surprisingly, the horses then all took the bundles in their mouths, lowered them from their backs to the ground and piled them all right there. The deer then took them in its mouth and took them back into the cave. Seeing that this was done, the horses seemed to sigh with relief and turned back to the road by which they had come.

The man, with wide eyes, now turned his attention to the cave and, with no fear of the dark, followed the deer deep into the interior. As he quickly went along, the place suddenly became shiningly bright and up ahead there was a large wide room, gradually elevated toward the back. To the man's surprise, a boy of six or seven was seated in the highest place, wearing a black headpiece and a bright green robe.

"Aha!" the man thought. "This must be the child concealing the god."

As he gazed steadily ahead, the deer skillfully brought in the bundles carried by the horses in its mouth and, taking out rice and salt they contained, began to prepare a meal. Then, in no time at all, kindling was fired up right before his eyes and a pot and pan began boiling away. The deer's dexterity with its hooves and mouth was beyond words.

Very soon, the rice was ready. A single small chirping bird appeared, perhaps from the ceiling, flew into the burning fire and was burned up.

A voice was then heard from the boy's mouth, "Little bird, for my sake you have become a dish to be eaten with my rice. I am so sorry." And the voice was the one he had heard coming from the god that day.

"The god! After all!" the man shouted and shook with emotion. "I've found him at last!"

The young boy, or rather the god, spoke as he ate the meal of fried bird the deer had put before him.

"I have no other choice about the form in which I appear in the world. Currently, I am being pursued by traitors and so have come to hide in this place. But the animals—this little bird, the deer and the horses are, needless to say, my allies. The animals will not betray me. And more, they would give up their lives for me . . . Do you see?" And, shedding tears, he pointed to the little bird on his plate.

Hearing the word "traitors," the man was at a loss and asked, "Honored God, who are these traitors?"

"False gods and those who believe in them," the god answered. "But their power will not endure for long. People like you who have deep faith are increasing and the traitors' retreat is just a matter of time." And again, he shed tears.

"Do not speak of this to anyone," the god said in a stern manner. "And do not come back here again."

"No," the man responded promptly. "Never again."

"Well then, you should go home. I'll have the deer send you off." And he gave the animal a wink.

When the man left the cave, the deer showed him the way and he returned to his village without incident.

This is the full story of a man who saw a god. After that, no one saw the god's form ever again.

Butchi-sama and the Temple Guardian Gods

These days there are few Buddhist image makers who carve statues of Kannon (the goddess of Mercy), or Nio (the temple guardian gods). But when faith in the Buddha was widespread, temples were established here and there, and many Buddhist image carvers went about the entire country reducing themselves to skin and bone doing such work. The work is different from that of a carpenter, as the carver must feel as though he is putting his own soul into the labor. This, then, is the strange story of the soul of a carver being lodged in a pair of temple guardian gods.

One thousand three hundred years ago, a large temple, the Gandenji, was established close to the Omi River in Sakakita.

"Goodness! Such a huge temple to be built in a country place like this!" the villagers exclaimed as they gathered together, unable to suppress feelings of both surprise and pride.

At any rate, the temple, built on a broad piece of land, had a beautiful dark roof and, at the entrance, a gate made with exquisite thick pillars for the two temple guardian gods. In the main hall, there were any number of gold shining Buddhist statues of Dainichi Nyorai, Bishamonten and the like, all carved by men summoned from the capital, Kyoto.

Even before the main hall was erected, the Buddhist image carvers put on fastidious looks as they worked hard, while people watched from a distance.

However, a young image carver who was working on statues of Nio, the two temple guardian gods, put down his chisel and mallet in an agreeable manner as he took a rest and spoke with the villagers himself.

"Hello there, barefooted kid . . ." he might call out to a

child without straw sandals who had come up close to watch. Once, he had given the children some rice crackers and after that they would noisily approach him.

"These are the number one rice crackers in the capital," he would tell them, dividing up the crackers and giving them out.

"The number one?"

"The number one?! Are they tasty?"

As the children talked together, the image carver would laugh, cock his head to one side and say, "The number one horrible. They have a terrible reputation." And laugh all the more in a great loud voice. "They're so bad that the shop owner couldn't sell them. I felt sorry for him and bought all the leftovers."

This man was so sweet-tempered that the children felt affectionate toward him, took him as being different from the other image carvers and called him Butchi-sama (an affectionate name for *busshi* "Buddhist image carver").

This image carver of the temple guardian gods was such a gentle-hearted man, but when he turned to the gods he was carving and took up his chisel, he appeared to be a completely different person. At such times, even the children would become quiet and watch intently. Yet when they saw the Butchi-sama was taking a break, they would immediately gather around him.

"Butchi-sama, tell us about the capital," they would clamor.

"Well now," he would say and, taking a deep breath, would tell them fanciful stories. "In the capital there is a beautiful princess who came from the Ryugu Palace, home of Ryu-O, the Dragon King..."

Then, after telling them such stories, Butchi-sama would continue working even when darkness fell, and finally completed carving the bodies of the two temple guardian gods. After that, he applied the colors of certain pigments and, taking special care with the vermilion, completed one of the figures.

"All right!"

Butchi-sama held his breath as he finished applying the

pigments to the first beautiful, sturdy temple guardian god while assessing it himself.

But, when he began to paint the second guardian god . . .

"Ah!" he yelled out, noticing that of the vermilion that he had prepared to use, only a little was left. He knew that this was not something that someone would have carried away, and so held his head in his hands and let out a deep sigh. He also knew that this pigment was not something he could get his hands on again in this rural area.

Thinking that the other Buddhist image carvers here for the work might have some themselves, he asked around, but was told, "You have been playing up to the villagers, so you must have some good idea." They had always been jealous of him and wouldn't give him any of the color even if they had it.

Butchi-sama anxiously checked once more what he had brought with him. But in the end he could find nothing.

"Ahh, I'll have to go to the capital," he sighed, and slumped down in a heap.

It was the end of autumn and snow was already falling in the nearby mountains. And with this, in order to go up to the capital, he would be crossing fields and mountains and would surely encounter blizzards. Yet, he was determined to make the trip.

"I'll be coming back in the spring of next year," he said to the villagers he had come to know. And to the children that heard this he entreated them over and over not to touch the temple guardian gods until he returned. Then he left.

Feeling sorry at his leaving, the children followed him to the pass just outside the village.

"Be sure to come back . . . Be sure!" they shouted, waving their hands. "And bring back some souvenirs! And say hello to the princess!"

With such calls while they could still see him, his figure disappeared into the crags and cliffs.

Butchi-sama made his journey, keeping the voices of the children as a prize in his heart. However, on his way, he gradually began to worry about the temple guardian gods, whose work he had given up on. On days of storms, on days of fair weather, or when lying down to rest in the grass, he would be consumed by feelings of regret and his eyes would fill up with tears.

And the children, for their part, would often go to the temple, look at the pair of unfinished guardian gods, and think of Butchi-sama.

        ◊   ◊   ◊

The months passed, but Butchi-sama did not return in the spring as he had promised. The heat of the summer arrived, but even then, Butchi-sama did not come back, and in the end, the children could stand it no longer.

"Butchi-sama, have you forgotten us?" they cried, and impatiently shook the temple guardian gods.

Gata gata, gata gata, gata gata . . .

The rocking back and forth gradually became greater and greater.

Unaware of this and still in the capital, Butchi-sama had finally obtained the vermilion paint he needed. Wanting to return as fast as he could, he hurried out on the road. And after a long, long journey, he at last reached the pass bordering the village. However, his body was now wasted, his eyes had become hollow and he was completely worn out.

"If I go around that rocky place . . . the temple . . . I can see the children . . ." But with these thoughts, he collapsed and his consciousness dimmed. At the same time, he began to feel sick, and though he tried, was unable to get up. But not only that, his entire body began to shake . . . *gata gata, gata gata, gata gata . . .* And at that moment, he could clearly see the vision of the temple guardian gods shaking back and forth.

"Ahh. Nio-sama . . . Nio-sama . . ."

But as he mouthed these words soundlessly, one of the villagers passed by. Breathing with difficulty, Butchi-sama gasped, "Please stop the shaking of the Nio-sama."

The villager did not understand what he meant, but went

straight away to the temple's Nio Gate, where he found the children rocking the statues of the temple guardian gods back and forth.

"Hey, hey! Stop it!" he yelled, explaining why to the children and some adults who had come up. They were all shocked and ran to the place where Butchi-sama was lying.

But there was no movement from Butchi-sama's body at all and he was no longer breathing. The people finally understood that there was a strange thread that connected the temple guardian gods and Butchi-sama's soul.

"Ahh, how heart-rending this is," they said, filled with grief. They buried Butchi-sama with great care. It was not just the children who loved Butchi-sama: everyone put their palms together in prayer at the grave and for a long time after spoke of Butchi-sama's soul being lodged in the Nio-sama.

And by the way, concerning the statue of the temple guardian god that Butchi-sama had left unpainted, somehow the vermilion color was coated onto it. Even if this was a miracle, the luster of the paint was still felt to be clearly different than it might have been, but it was left as it was.

The Great Rock and the Traveling Priest

In the castle, the lord let out a great yawn. The retainer who saw that called out, "The lord seems to be bored . . ."

"It's spring now. You know, I'd like to go out to the fields to see the flowers or the stones . . ."

"Ah, yes. The flowers and stones?"

"Yes. I especially like the stones."

And indeed, the castle garden was full of arranged stones.

At that, the retainer called up a number of people and went outside with the lord. Beyond the castle was a grassy plain and larks were singing in the sky. A pleasant wind brushed past their cheeks.

"My lord, flowers . . ."

The retainers amused their lord by holding the stems of dandelions and blowing their seeds away; and, finding some tulips, putting them in vases and holding them before him.

Each time, the lord would glance at them and laugh, "Well, well." But then he said, "I've had enough of flowers. Are there no stones?"

The retainers then looked around here and there, and when finding rare or strange ones would carry them back for the lord to see. Curved stones, stones with holes in them, stones shaped like boats—they brought and lined up many for him—but the lord said, "No, no. What I want is a large stone. I want to see a stone bigger than any in the castle."

Hearing this, the retainers replied, "All right. We'll have to go up to the mountain and look around. There will be some big ones there for sure."

They led him to the mountain, asking him if his legs would be all right, and being assured that they would be.

As the lord began to climb up a mountain path lined by forest, he suddenly turned back toward the left.

"That's the stone I want," he said, laughing. "It's shaped like a toad. How amusing!"

The retainers looked at the stone and were both shocked and confused. To bring back that huge stone would require at least five oxen pulling together.

"My lord, that's a bit . . ." the head of the retainers mumbled, trying to appease him, but the lord insisted.

There was nothing to be done, so one of them ran back to the castle as a messenger and returned with a hundred retainers, a thick coil of rope and two horses. They then wrapped up the stone with the rope and began pulling.

This huge stone was situated on a slope, so when aimed toward the castle, it tumbled down rather easily and arrived at the foot of the slope. From there, everyone, dripping in sweat, pulled along with the horses.

But although they were able to pull the stone as far as the entrance to the village, for some reason they were able to go no farther.

"Well, here's trouble!"

"The stone itself must be in a bad mood."

While they spoke together like this, an evening breeze wafted in.

"I'll ask you again later," the lord said and returned to the castle. A little after that, a messenger came from the castle, with the following pronouncement:

"The lord is quite angry. He says that if you are not able to finish this work by the time the moon rises, everyone will be beheaded."

When they heard this, the retainers were struck by fear. The lord had always been capricious and would say such things from time to time.

The sun was already slanted toward the west and its light beginning to weaken.

"Beheaded! Beheaded!"

"Ahh, and I still have a young child and a wife."

"Tomorrow is my daughter's wedding."

The retainers all spoke together and spilled out their resentment toward the lord, while there were others who threw themselves down crying, no longer having the energy to pull the stone.

But then the head of the retainers said, "Look, it doesn't do any good to cry. This is the fate of those who serve this lord. Let's see what we can do."

The head retainer encouraged them all to get back on their feet. But the big stone would not move a bit, and the horses whinnied in pain.

Just at that moment, a traveling priest approached them.

"What's happening? What is so distressing that everyone is crying?" he asked soothingly.

"Well, the fact is . . ." and the head of the retainers explained the situation.

The priest listened carefully and said, "That's nothing so bad that you have to cry about it." And, with a short pause, he looked at them all and spoke calmly.

"This stone has been cursed and is not likely to budge. But if a sutra is quietly intoned, it should move, I suppose."

Saying this, the priest sat on the ground in front of the stone and putting the palms of his hands together, began to intone the Buddhist chant, "Namu Amida Butsu, Namu Amida Butsu . . ."

Taking his example, the retainers also sat down and began to chant, "Namu Amida Butsu . . ."

Just at that point, the big stone began to shake unsteadily and it seemed that it would move right away.

"Yaa! It's moving, it's moving!"

Everyone was astonished and stood up, while the horses pulled and the stone began to move quickly along as though logs had been placed beneath it. In this way, they were able to pull the stone into the castle grounds by the time the sun set.

"Hey! What happened to that priest?" someone said. As they looked around, they all realized that the priest was nowhere to be seen.

The story was then told to the lord, who was not only surprised but impressed, and said, "Huh. Namu Amida Butsu?"

After that, he worshipped the Buddha fervently and never
said anything capricious again.

Or so it is said.

PART 10

LIVING BEINGS THAT BECAME APPARITIONS

Conchs, Parent and Child

With their attractive, rounded shape, conchs give an impression of being gentle and simple, but in fact, when need be, they are quite scary.

In a certain place, there was once a lone hunter. This man would go out to the mountains every day and chase down wild beasts. But one day, he was not able to take even a single rabbit.

"What in the world is going on?" he wondered. He had chased the animals around without even eating his lunch and was by this time panting and exhausted. Seeing that the sun was now inclining toward the west and thinking it was time to collect himself, he sat down to rest at the root of a tree and started to eat the rice balls he'd brought with him.

Then, seeming to hear a high-pitched voice, he quickly turned his head in surprise. And there, right before his eyes, was that not a small conch springing about in play?

"Huh, a conch on this kind of mountain?" he said to himself, gazing at the conch in surprise. "All right then. I'll take it to show everyone in the village."

With this in mind, he took off his undershirt, grabbed the little conch and wrapped it up in it. But then, from within the wrapping, he heard the sound of something crying.

"Well then, I've not only captured this thing, but can even hear it crying," he laughed, tying the conch wrapped up in his undershirt to the branch of a nearby tree. Shouldering his gun and standing up, he coldly murmured, "So wait there. I've got something else to do." He turned toward the interior of the mountain and went off in search of game.

The sky, however, suddenly clouded over and as his surroundings turned dark, a heavy rain began to fall in ribbons.

"Huh! And it was such a clear day until now."

The man resentfully wrung out his thoroughly soaked

shirt and, wiping the rain off his neck, retreated to the place he had been.

Just at that time, the mountain around him began to crumble with a thudding sound and the nearby waterfall began to overflow with a power that threatened to swallow him up. With a cry, the frightened man untied the wrapped-up conch from the branch and fled down the mountain holding it. But with a great rumble, a flood chased after him.

Panting heavily, he arrived at his house, but found that the water had already reached it and there was no way to get inside. From somewhere he could hear a strange blowing noise.

There was nothing the man could do and he quickly hurried up the hill behind the house. Finally, just as he was composing himself a little and looking at the muddy water flowing right before his eyes, he let out a yell. A large conch, as big as a cauldron, was flowing down the mountain floodwaters still making a blowing sound. And right behind it was a small conch happily bobbing up and down.

With a start, the man looked at the undershirt he had been holding that contained the conch. At some point, a hole had opened up in it and the conch was not there.

"So that's it, so that's it," said the man, realizing that it had been the conch's parent that had caused the flood and come to take back its child.

A parent may be like this.

The man forgot about his flooded house and prayed that the parent and child would return safely to the sea.

The White Horse That Disappeared into the Evening Sky

There once was a horse market at the An'genji Temple in northern Shinano that was quite famous. Every November, a great number of horses were brought here from the neighboring villages.

"Well now, well now. Its mane, the look of its hooves, the look of its eyes—you won't get another deal like this no matter where you go." With such lively talk, the horses were bought and sold.

Now, one year there was a farmer who could not make up his mind whether to put up his horse for sale or not. The year before, this farmer's house had been damaged by the flooding of the Chikuma River, the produce of his rice paddies and vegetable fields had all been washed away and, existing on nothing more than rice gruel, he was finally unable to make a living.

At his house, there remained only one white horse, and the farmer's only son, Sasuke, loved the horse and rode it here and there. Knowing that they couldn't afford to keep it, Sasuke's father and mother were constantly distressed.

The night before the horse market, the father said sadly that, after all, they would have to sell Ao, the horse. At which, Sasuke threw his bowl of rice gruel across the room and sobbed, "No, Father, please don't! Without Ao, I will die."

"But, you know . . ." Sasuke's father and mother looked at each other, biting their lips.

"That's enough. How many times have I heard this . . ." and Sasuke abruptly leapt up and ran outside.

"Sasuke! Listen, Sasuke!" His mother ran after him in a panic, but Sasuke did not come back.

The next day the farmer could think of nothing but the situation with Sasuke, going over it again and again in his head, but in the end, with tears in his eyes, he led Ao to the horse market. When he arrived at the market grounds, there were a number of horses being auctioned around the temple bell tower and under a tall ginkgo tree. Letting out a heavy sigh, he said, "Excuse me," and led the horse forward.

At that point, everyone's eyes were fixed on Ao at once. Its mane was beautiful and its hooves lovely, they said amongst themselves in admiration. It was a horse that anyone who saw it would want, and people gathered around it very quickly.

"How about it? I'll give you anything you want. Will you sell it to me?"

Someone else came forward from the sidelines and called out, "Don't be foolish! Hand it over to me!" Then, just a though a dam had broken, one man after another raised the price in a loud babble of voices.

Just at that moment, someone burst in through the crowd. It was Sasuke.

"Ah! Sasuke . . . it's you . . ."

While his father stood there in surprise, Sasuke mounted the white horse.

"This horse will not be sold to anyone!" he yelled and kicked Ao's ribcage with both feet. The horse immediately took off and leapt outside of the auction grounds, while the others looked on in blank amazement,

"Sasuke!" his father cried. But with Sasuke mounted on its back, the white horse suddenly soared up into the sky and, after circling the market grounds, disappeared into the faraway evening glow in the twinkling of an eye.

It was something that happened in a moment and was as beautiful as a painting.

After that, Sasuke and the horse never returned.

The Cat That Went into a Painting

In the Kokugonji Temple in Nakano, there is a painting of the Buddha. It is called a "painting of the Buddha," but for some reason, there is a cat seated right in its center.

Here is the explanation.

One day, a famous traveling artist of Buddhist paintings arrived unexpectedly at the temple. At this sudden visit, the priest exclaimed his admiration for the man, invited him inside and served him tea. And in his heart was just one thought: there are no good illustrations of the Buddha in this temple. Perhaps the artist would be kind enough to paint one.

And so, with great deference, he made this request.

"Please. We will remunerate you as you wish."

"If that's the case, I will paint one for you, but to do this, I will need to stay here for a number of nights. Is that all right with you?"

And with that, the artist put down his bags and settled into the temple.

But the artist either played with a stray cat, Tora, that had made the temple its home during the day, or did nothing but sleep and never took up his paintbrush. The priest felt uneasy about this, but one night the artist sat down before a large sheet of paper in the main hall.

When three days had passed, one could see something like a rough sketch of the Buddha.

"Ah, this is wonderful!" the priest sighed in relief as he gazed at the work.

However, Tora was always sitting next to the artist when he held his brush. And no, it would have been fine if the cat had just been sitting there, but it also played with the brush or scratched its nails on the artist's back. The priest could not stand to see this and so, picking up Tora, did his best to keep the cat from coming into the main hall. But even then, the cat wanted in and would not be enclosed. Finally, the priest tied it to a pillar with a string, but even that did no good.

The artist, as one might have expected, just laughed and said, "I don't mind if it just wants to play."

The cat eventually became rather bold and even scratched the face of the Buddha, which had been painted in detail. And at that, even the artist turned pale and thought, "Tora, why are you so discontented?" And at this, the cat sat down in the middle of the painting and meowed, looking at the artist's face.

The artist stroked its head and muttered, "I've never seen this kind of cat before," and turned it over on its back.

At this, the cat took the paintbrush in its mouth, climbed onto the artist's stomach and seemed to gesture for him to paint, paint.

"Ahh, All right. I understand!" the artist said and sat up straight. Then, taking the brush that was still in the cat's mouth, began to vigorously paint Tora, not in the center of the almost-finished work but in the corner. The cat then, making a strange sound, jumped around in pleasure.

"Aha! That's it, that's it," the artist exclaimed and firmly painted the figure of a seated Tora.

When the painting was finished, the priest came in, listened to what had happened, and exclaimed happily, "Is that so? What an unusual painting."

This is the story behind the Buddhist painting in this temple. Cats are something like demons, and this is a story that is difficult to understand.

The Kitsune's Rice-Planting

The fox demons known as Kitsune also like to try their hand at rice-planting.

Long ago, there was a female Kitsune, Ochiyo, that lived deep in Mount Hotaka, and when it was time for rice-planting, Ochiyo went down to the village and watched the people planting rice seedlings.

"I'd like to do that, too," she murmured, and returned to the mountain.

When Ochiyo happened to mention this by chance to an elderly Kitsune, the latter advised the younger Kitsune to go try it. When the season arrived for rice-planting the following year, Ochiyo went down to the village as the elderly Kitsune had advised.

"Well, if I'm going to plant rice seedlings with them, I would like to do it with a handsome, easygoing young man," said Ochiyo, as she looked down from a fairly high hill for a while. As she did this, she noticed a lone man planting rice seedlings and dripping with sweat.

"All right. That's the right man," she thought, and changed her body into the form of a young woman. Then, just to make sure, she went down next to the man's rice field. The man did not notice her but continued working hard.

At that point, the Kitsune—now appearing as a young woman—was resolved and spoke up with an "Excuse me."

Wiping off his sweat, the man looked up. As you might think, he was surprised at seeing a beautiful woman he had never noticed before standing there. The woman said, "I have come to attempt rice-planting. Would you let me try, please?"

At this, the man was surprised a second time.

"What did you say just now?"

"Rice-planting. I asked if you would let me try."

The man looked carefully at the beautiful kimono the woman was wearing.

"A kimono like that will soon be covered in mud. So, you're asking too much," he laughed. The woman was so beautiful that this was all he could think of to say.

At that, the woman tucked up the skirt of her kimono and, with her sleeves rolled up, looked at the way the man was planting the seeds and, imitating him, began to work.

When the man saw this, he was completely astonished. "Well, I'm amazed," he said. "Are you the daughter of some farmer? What is your name?"

The woman laughed softly and replied, "My name is Ochiyo. I was born on the other side of the mountain. So, what is your name?"

"Me? My name is Heikichi and I live alone."

With this back and forth, the rice-planting went on agreeably and they both got into a good mood. By evening, they had completely planted all the seedlings in three rice fields and Heikichi, with some embarrassment asked, "If you would like, would you become my wife?"

Ochiyo answered without hesitation, "Ahh, that would be very nice."

And with this beginning, the two became man and wife.

Ochiyo did the laundry, was talented at cooking, good at putting the house in order; and gained fame in the neighborhood. She became so fond of Heikichi that she had no desire to return to the mountain.

☖   ☖   ☖

Before long a child was born, which was nurtured on its mother's milk and grew up quickly. But after a while, it was no longer necessary to feed milk to the child. One day, in the winter, the brazier was bright red with a burning fire. Ochiyo held the child that had grown heavy, when she started to feel drowsy. Heikichi was weaving straw rope next to her and began to speak.

"Hey, Ochiyo . . ."

Then, "What is this?" Wasn't that a brown tail coming from Ochiyo's behind?

A Kitsune . . . ?

"This just can't be," he thought, but looked again and again and, sure enough, it was a Kitsune's tail.

Heikichi's mind went completely blank. He put down the straw rope, went into the bedroom and, lying on his back, calmed himself down. "Ochiyo is a Kitsune . . . but I love her. And we even have a child. Ahh . . ."

After that, while Heikichi was aware of her true form, he said nothing about it but continued to love her as before. And in the meanwhile, he saw her tail a number of times, but acted as though he had not seen it at all. Of course, he did not expose this secret to anyone in the village.

The child grew up to be a strong, healthy man. A baby girl born after him grew up to be quite beautiful. Ochiyo and Heikichi both took on years, and while lying next to each other in bed would often talk about the time they met.

"You were such a good man, I quickly came to you as a wife," Ochiyo said.

"Of course, you were the only one for me," Heikichi gently replied to her.

Some time later, their son, realizing that the villagers were in desperate need of water, dug a number of canals and a well, pleasing everyone. About the daughter, nothing is known, but no one was ever aware that the two were created from the blood of a Kitsune.

The Korokoro Obake

There are many kinds of Obake in this world, and the Obake in the village of Nakahata was evil in this way:

This being a village, there was a shrine surrounded by a forest. To get to the neighboring village you would take a by-road, but at night you would always hear a rolling sound coming from behind you,

Korokoro...

And if there was only this rolling sound, you could put up with it, but the little pebbles beneath your feet would roll too as though they were crawling.

Even if the villagers had some business to carry out in the next village, they would do it during the daytime and disliked traveling after dark. Nevertheless, there were always errands that needed to be done at night, and the only path to the next village was this one.

"It will be all right if the Obake appears," the villagers said among themselves. "Just carry a cleaver." They wondered what the Obake looked like and whether anyone would find out. But there was no one brave enough to do this.

In the meantime, there was not only the *korokoro*, but now the sound of something like a rock being thrown. By this point the villagers were afraid that they might be abducted by this Obake. And just as this talk had become the sole topic of conversation, a traveler came by. He was an old man and did not look like he might be of assistance, but when he heard the story, he laughed.

"Well now, how interesting," he said, and offered to undertake the job of subduing the Obake.

The villagers all looked at each other and cried, "Really?"

"And what about remuneration?" one man asked.

The old man laughed and declared he wanted nothing.

Well, that night, the man went immediately to the shrine

and then walked any number of times over the road where the villagers thought the ghost was. And from behind him came the sound, *korokoro*, and small stones rolled in front of him. In his heart he cried out and he broke into a run. At the same time, stones flew at him, and the more he ran, the more stones came flying.

He turned and shouted "More, more . . . ," deliberately inviting even more stones to be thrown.

In response, the stones flew fast and furious, but then they gradually decreased and the sound of heavy breathing was coming from somewhere. Hearing this, the man responded, "What's this? It's not right for an Obake to be such a coward!"

Larger stones began to fly at him, but the Obake still could not be seen. "And what's this? Why such little stones?"

When he had responded to big stones flying at him a number of times, he finally caught sight of his opponent in the light of the moon—it was a little Tanuki raccoon-dog yokai holding a big stone, groaning and out of breath. Finally, with a grunt, it threw the stone.

The man approached the Tanuki. "Look!" he said. "If you're a Tanuki, you should climb up a sturdy tree and throw down a bigger stone. Do you understand?" he continued. "It's no good if a Tanuki can't shape itself into something more like a real Tanuki. You haven't had enough training."

At these stern words, the Tanuki began to cry.

"This kind of spooking," the man went on, "brings shame upon Tanuki. Go back to the mountains, get more practice, then come around."

"Yes, I'll do that," the Tanuki sobbed.

Hearing this, the man quickly spoke in a gentle voice, "But I'm relieved knowing you're alive. Everyone was worried that you were dead. And doing this shabby spooking in a place like this."

With a hint of suspicion, the Tanuki looked through its tears once again at the man. Then, the clouds parted and the moon showed its face.

"What?" it yelled, facing the man. "You're really the old Tanuki from Shigurezawa!"

"Ha, ha, ha," the man laughed. "So, you know now. I took
on the form of a human being and walked out here looking
for you because I was worried."

"I'm so sorry," the Tanuki replied.

"Well, now everyone will be relieved. Keep this as a lesson. The next time I come, I'll show you much better ways of
spooking people. What do you think?"

"Oh, yes!"

The man then retreated down the road he had come by
during the day, but now in the light of the moon.

And after that there were no more spooky sounds of
korokoro or of striking stones, or even stories of other ghosts
passing through.

The Ox's Love

If animals like monkeys and horses have affection toward human beings, then so do oxen.

In the village of Yamada in northern Shinano, there was a village headman whose family kept a black male ox. The one who loved this animal more than anyone was the headman's only daughter, Kayo. When Kayo accompanied the ox to the fields, plowing the rice paddies or carrying lading, it seemed to feel happy and worked hard. And, when taking a break, she would not tie it to a tree, but would let it go free, and found it well-behaved and gentle. Not only that, but when it nestled close to Kayo's head, she treated it like a baby, stroking its head.

"There, there, now . . ."

But what drove the ox mad was talk of Kayo's getting married. It would rampage about and snort in a strange way.

Kayo saw through what was in its heart. "Now, now, don't be upset. Everything is all right," she said.

The day finally arrived when Kayo was to go to the nearby village to become a bride. That evening, she went to the shed, caressed the ox and was about to tell it that they would be separated.

"It's been wonderful," she said, looking in the direction of the ox, "but now I must say goodbye."

With that, the ox, which had been lying down in the rear of the shed, got up stolidly and drew near to Kayo. Kayo now saw the brand new saddle that was to be used for her wedding on its back.

"Yes!" she said without thinking, "I'm going to mount on this and go." And then, "Be calm. Your heart is pounding."

From that moment, she relaxed and made her way through the entry bar of the stall.

"All right. I'm mounting up!" And with that, she climbed

up onto its back. At that moment the ox went wild, broke through the stall bar and charged outside.

Kayo screamed and fell off the ox to the ground. As her mother rushed to her, Kayo's breast was pierced by one of the ox's horns, and her blood began to flow.

Naturally, her family and the villagers as well were thrown into an uproar.

"That vicious animal!"

The most upset was the headman. "This shameless ox has done this right before her wedding! I'm going to kill it!" he cried, mad with anger, and the commotion became all the greater. People drew near with hoes and thick logs and began to beat the ox with all their strength, yelling for it to die. But no matter how much it was beaten and injured, the ox stamped its hooves and did not move.

"What is this?" the people shouted, their arms hurting from beating the animal, and their hands covered in blood. "It's pouring with blood, but still won't move." Eventually, they all gave up and stopped to catch their breath.

But just as Kayo's mother passed by carrying the dead body of her daughter, the ox's legs gave out, and it fell to the ground, where it breathed its last. Tears had been flowing from its eyes.

In the end, people finally understood the ox's feelings and carefully buried it next to Kayo's grave.

PART 11

THE STRANGENESS OF SUPERNATURAL BEINGS

The Story of Mount Garyu

A long, long time ago, a priest came from far away to the village of Suzaka.

Just before the village was the Sakata Pass. When the priest climbed up the road to the pass, he stopped to catch his breath and looking over the broad plain and the mountains beyond, said, quite beside himself, "What beautiful scenery! That must be Mount Togakushi. And next to it, perhaps Mount Iizuna . . ."

Below him, he could see a large meandering river, shining brightly in the summer light, and people working in the rice paddies and fields.

"Hmm. Well then . . . what about the temple I'm looking for? Where could it be?"

His eyes scanned the scene before him. "Ah!" he muttered, "That must be it. That big . . . What the . . . ?" And he cocked his head to one side. He felt that the large black forest next to the temple was somehow moving.

And just as he said, "It must be my imagination," the forest suddenly lifted up and moved.

In the midst of his surprise, the forest turned into the form of a large dragon, spitting flames from its mouth and raising its head in his direction.

The priest yelled out and involuntarily fell back on his buttocks. Then the dragon raised its head up to the sky.

"Gyaa!" it howled, and at the same time shook its tail back and forth raising a windstorm as it flew into the air. At this terrible disturbance, the villagers could be seen running around in fright.

"This is not right," the priest muttered to himself. "I must calm that dragon."

Refraining from going on to the temple he had had his eye

on, the priest meditated on what he should do. After a while, he set down his travel pack. Taking out some carving tools, he resignedly began to engrave something into the large rock at his side.

"If I don't do this," he mumbled as he chiseled, "that violent dragon will not be pacified." And then he shouted, "All right! Here goes!"

In the meantime, the dragon was battering down things, and looked as though it was coming to attack the village.

Night had fallen as the priest had been chiseling on the rock. Nevertheless, he continued his work while camping outside. Gradually, the clouds began to clear and the stars to shine. The priest kept on at his chiseling, and the wriggling dragon's strength began to weaken.

"Ah! Done!" the priest exclaimed, and facing the engraved rock, put his hands together in prayer. On the face of the rock, the priest had carved the kanji character 龍, which means "dragon" and as the character had taken shape, the dragon's movements and even its breath had weakened.

This kanji character for dragon had the power of a charm or incantation.

When the priest finished his prayer, a whirlwind rose up, took the entire rock flying into the sky, and with a great crash let it fall upon the dragon's head. In that instant, the dragon screamed with a sound that seemed as though heaven and earth were being rent apart, and the dragon breathed its last. The dragon then lay on its side, stock still, and hardened into a small mountain.

During the dragon's rampage, the places on the land that had been scratched by its claws became hollows, and, as time passed and with the villagers' efforts, became beautiful ponds overflowing with water. Then, after a long time, cherry trees bloomed alongside of the ponds, and on the mountain where the dragon's body had been, a forest of tall trees grew, providing a place where people came to rest.

Nowadays, it remains a mystery as to what happened to the priest after these events or to the rock that danced into the sky.

But the story is still handed down that the rock is buried somewhere on the mountain, now called Mount Garyu, which means the Mountain of the Reclining Dragon.

The Children Snatched Away by the Demon

"What? Your child is gone, too?"

"Yes, since last night."

"My child, too. What's happening?"

This kind of talk quickly circulated in the village of Chino, as the number of children that had disappeared rose to nine. The villagers all searched high and low together, but without any success.

One day, Heizo, the four-year-old child of Gengoro, a skillful stonemason, suddenly could not be found. The evening that Heizo disappeared, Gengoro went out to the bamboo thicket behind the house and discovered what looked like the footprints of an Oni demon.

Gengoro turned pale. He remembered that Heizo had been in the thicket that day, looking for insects. Unable to work, he and his wife went out looking for him and calling his name until the stars began to shine. But they were unable to find him.

Both husband and wife were so worried about their son, that they were unable to eat.

"The key to this puzzle must be those Oni footprints . . ."

"If he was abducted by an Oni, even Kintoki, the great guardian god of Mount Oe, would be unable to help us."

"Ten children have been kidnapped until now."

"But no one even seems to be upset any more. Maybe they've given up."

As Gengoro and his wife spoke in this way, a year went by. Then one day they heard a rumor that an Oni had flown from Mount Tateshina toward Hiromi Pass and this, along with the earlier sighting of the Oni's footprint, brought them to the heart-rending conclusion that their son was no longer alive. They thought about holding a funeral service for him.

Gengoro felt that he wanted at least to carve a statue of the bodhisattva Jizo at Hiromi Plain where they could pray and, shouldering his equipment, he trudged along out in search of a good rock. At last, he found an excellent round rock a little distance away. When he approached it through the pampas grass, he put down the chisel and mallet he had brought with him, put his hands together and, facing the rock, prayed to be able to carve a good Jizo.

Finally, Gengoro struck the rock with the mallet with all his might and a great echo resounded throughout the place.

"Still, why do I have to do this?" he thought, tears flowing from his eyes.

But to his surprise, with the second strike of the mallet, it seemed that a strange sound rang out. He put his ear to the rock and felt that he could hear something like the commotion of a child's voice.

"What on earth . . . ?"

Inclining his head and taking a breath, he hit the rock with a clang once more; and sure enough, with this, the sound of children's voices echoed out. And amongst these voices, Gengoro felt that he could hear the voice of Heizo. Wiping off his sweat, he continued carving, but every time he swung his mallet, he could hear the voices.

"Surely, if I can finish carving the statue, I will understand the secret of all this," he thought, and continued carving even after the sun had set and the stars were shining in the sky. No matter how tired he became, he did not rest, or even stop to eat. Wanting only to hear Heizo's voice, he pounded clang, clang with his mallet and pressed his ear to the rock. But that was not enough, and finally he put his mouth to the rock and called, "Heizo! Heizo!"

Yet, there was no answer. Regardless, he carried on with his work, putting into it all of his spirit. Gradually, the statue of Jizo took shape. And as it did, the voices of the children inside the rock started to sound full of joy.

"All right! I'm going to rescue you!" shouted Gengoro, forgetting about the weakened state of his body. He continued his carving, working by firelight through the nights.

At last, the night of the fifth day came.

"Done!" he exclaimed, and completely collapsed. Breathing heavily, he shut his eyes and put his hands together in prayer. "Honorable Jizo. Ahh . . ."

Suddenly, a commanding voice seemed to come from above, "Become a lion! Become a tiger!"

Struggling to his feet, Gengoro looked toward the sky. The voice came, once again. "Become a lion! Become a tiger!"

Gengoro felt that this had come from Jizo's mouth and, without thinking, straightened his posture and put his hands together in prayer. Then, from Jizo's mouth, which was illuminated by the bonfire, came these clear words, "Right! From now on, it's a battle. You'll become a lion. You'll become a tiger. No matter what kind of frightening thing occurs, you will fight and not run away."

"Yes, Honorable Jizo."

Hanging his head, Gengoro recalled the rumors of the Oni. "But will I be fighting an Oni?"

He had no idea from where the Oni might come and was at a loss. Jizo again spoke up.

"You have offered prayers, but the Oni has enclosed the children in this rock. But now that you have carved my likeness, the Oni is frightened and confused and in a state of madness. Still, the children are brave and have started to attack it."

"What?!"

"That's right," Jizo continued, "The Oni is about to fly out. Be ready!"

At this, shouting and yelling voices came from within the rock, which began to shake and finally broke into pieces as a huge red Oni, looking horribly pained, flew out. With his mallet, Gengoro struck the Oni's head. With the power of the blow, the Oni cried out and fell to the ground. In that instant, the children appeared, full of energy and high spirits.

When he saw Heizo among them, he cried out, "Ahh, Honorable Jizo . . ."

Jizo and the rock, however, were in pieces, and his image was completely gone.

Heizo called his father's name and ran to hug him. As Gengoro embraced his son, he looked at the other happy children and thought how strange all this was.

In the meantime, the day began to break and the sun shone down on the place and as they all calmed down, their eyes fell on the collapsed Oni, which was breathing its last. As its blood flowed, its body faded and finally became nothing but pebbles.

Gengoro and the children prayed in front of the crushed Jizo. Gengoro said softly, "All is well, all is well. These children were saved by the honorable Jizo. So, we will never forget to come here to bring flowers in offering."

This story continued to be told long after Gengoro passed away. And in particular, the place where the Oni's blood flowed was given the name Blood Plain (Chinohara), written with the kanji character for blood 血, pronounced *chi*. Nowadays, however, it is written with the character 茅, meaning pampas grass, but also pronounced *chi*.

The Haunted Temple

Obake ghosts often appear in temples that have no priest, and it was well-known that Obake appeared unusually often at a certain temple in northern Shinano.

Because these Obake haunted the place, the priests would not stay long there and, over the generations, it had become completely abandoned. No one would go in to take care of the garden, which became rank with weeds, and the villagers never went near the place. And if children cried, their parents would say things like, "Listen, the Obake at the temple is going to come for you," or "You're going to bring on the Obake," while trying to calm them down.

♦　♦　♦

Now one autumn day, there was a funeral in the village, but there was no one to chant the sutras.

"We have a temple, but no priest," said the villagers among themselves. "Could we be sending the deceased to Hell?"

As the family and relatives knit their brows in sorrow, a black robed priest peeped into the house of the deceased and asked what was the matter. Everyone expressed their joy in one voice at this development, invited the priest in, explained the matter, and the funeral was completed.

When the funeral was over, the priest heard the story of the haunted temple in detail.

"All right," he said with full confidence. "I'm going to take care of it."

The priest was quite stout and dignified, and everyone bowed down to him in supplication. But they soon realized he was just an easygoing priest who would stop over at houses where there was a funeral, eat delicious food and do nothing

but sleep, and that he was not going to go out to defeat the Obake at all.

After a few days of lolling around and doing nothing, however, he finally got up and said, "All right! Tonight, I'll show you how to conquer the Obake. Please loan me a rolling pin," and with that, went off, carrying with him a long buckwheat noodle roller.

When the priest arrived at the temple, he lit a fire in the hearth in the priests' quarters that was covered with spiders' webs and waited, as he warmed himself, for an Obake to appear. But although he waited and waited, there was no Obake, and eventually he fell asleep.

Suddenly, the priest awoke, hearing a sound—*bari bari*—above his head, and saw something like a bat dropping down as if to cover the hearth. When the priest saw its glaring and shining eyes, he aimed at those eyes with the tip of the rolling pin and was about to strike. His opponent let out a scream and belched forth a bright red flame from its hatchet-shaped mouth, scorching the priest's face.

But the priest was not deterred. He stood facing the thing, roller in hand.

"Show your true form right now," he said.

His opponent made no response, and instead poised itself to launch another attack. Just at that point, the priest took a slip of paper from his robe and held it up to the Obake. The thing instantly fell to the floor with a thud and collapsed, completely flattened out.

"What's this? What a slovenly Obake!" the priest snorted; and when he looked carefully in the light of the fire, he saw that the Obake was a Tanuki raccoon-dog yokai, bleeding from its mouth.

"Now, now," said the priest, who came up to the Tanuki's side, helping it to sit up. "Here, wipe your mouth with this," he said, and offered it a hand towel.

The Tanuki took it furtively in both paws and wiped its mouth as it had been told.

"What a faker!" the priest laughed. "You're no good at all!"

He then preached a sermon and put the paper with Namu Amida Butsu inscribed in black ink at his side.

"No one can win against Namu Amida Butsu," he said, lying down next to the hearth. Soon he was snoring.

The next morning, the villagers were worried about what had happened to the priest, and went up to the temple, where they found him snoring away, sleeping soundly. Someone whispered in his ear, "Well . . . um . . . what happened about subduing the Obake?"

The priest got up and laughed. "It was nothing," he said. "It's all over."

"Then, what was the true form of the Obake?" asked the head of the household that had had the funeral. And the priest explained what had happened the night before. The strength of the Namu Amida Butsu chant impressed them especially, and they turned to the paper the priest held before them and chanted it, putting their hands together in prayer.

"You cannot ever be negligent about this powerful Buddhist chant," the priest said as he left the village. And from the forest on the hill just outside of the village, the Tanuki of the night before and its companions gazed at him as though sending him off.

After that, of course, there was never any more talk about Obake appearing at the temple. The people cleaned the place up, greeted a new priest and gathered there quite often. And the chanting—Namu Amida Butsu, Namu Amida Butsu—never ceased.

Frightening Hair

The overwhelming majority of Japanese people have black hair. But even now, there are some that are born with reddish brown or whitish hair. But these are very few.

Though they are few, there is no shame in this and they live to be very fine people. It is a sad thing, however, that long ago, children with different hair were discriminated against and often suffered.

In a certain village there was a woman by the name of O-tae. She had reddish hair from the time she was born and the neighborhood children taunted her, yelling, "Red, red, O-tae." Even the grown-ups said, "She's very pretty, but how sad . . ." because compared with the other children, her hair stood out.

Because she was kidded and teased so much, O-tae spent day after day crying, but one day, a girl called O-shin, who lived in the house next door, approached her and rather kindly whispered in her ear, "If you'd like for your hair to be black, go to the pool at the Nishino River on a moonlit night, and wash your hair there. From the time I was born, my mother always washed my hair there, and you can see how pretty it is now."

"Thank you," O-tae replied. "If I thought I'd have to spend my life with this hair, I'd die."

However, one month passed, and then two months went by, and her hair did not become even a bit black.

Her mother couldn't just stand by and watch this, and said to her daughter sadly, "O-shin has just fooled you. As your mother, I gave birth to you like this, but there's no way I can change the way you were born. You should give up on what O-shin told you to do and ask for help from the monk in the next village."

With tears in her eyes, her mother had the monk from the neighboring village come to visit.

The monk entered their house, looked at O-tae's hair and said, "This will never do. If you do not mend this, you will never get married." And he lit candles on either side of the household Buddhist altar. He then seated O-tae in front of the altar, waved a sacred wand in a dramatic fashion and started to pray.

After thoroughly performing this cleansing ceremony, the monk continued, "This will do. For three years and three months you will have some distress but be patient. When that time is over, your hair will definitely turn black."

This done, he received the fee from her mother and returned home.

"Ahh, another three years and three months," slipped inadvertently from the mouths of both O-tae and her mother. Nevertheless, O-tae continued in her belief that this would be true and waited for that day as though in a dream.

However, even when that day passed, her hair had not turned the least bit black. And all the other girls had begun to get married . . .

"Ahh, I've been fooled again," O-tae realized, and shed bitter tears. One night, she cut off her hair with scissors as though she had gone insane and, with specific bitter resentment toward O-shin, threw her hair into the pond at the Nishino River.

With this, the strands of hair twisted about together, moving as though alive and sank to the bottom of the pond. Then, to O-tae's shock, the hair that had sunk to the bottom now floated up to the surface and changed into numerous snakes. Crawling up to the bank of the pond, the snakes draped themselves around O-tae and laughed altogether.

"O-tae, why do you dislike us, your own hair, so much?"

"Eh! This should take care of you!"

"We're going to take you to the bottom of Hell!"

Making O-tae feel dizzy with their taunts, they pulled her into the pond.

"I'm sorry!" O-tae screamed. "I'm sorry!" Her voice echoed all around.

After that, an undetermined time passed, and a fisherman from the village found O-tae collapsed on the bank of the Nishino River. And thanks to him, she came to herself again.

After this, would O-tae ever been sad about her red hair again? Well, a young man appeared who could not have cared at all about the color of her hair and married her after all.

BAFFLING STORIES OF REMARKABLE PEOPLE

Master Genkaku of Aruga Pass

Long ago, there was a *yamabushi* mountain monk who settled in the Aruga Pass in Suwa. The villagers called him Genkaku-sama and felt a strong affection for him. This was because he would cure their illnesses and listen to them when they were troubled.

"How are things going? Are you well now?" he would call out as he walked about the houses, blowing his conch. In response, every house would offer him rice and vegetables, keeping up good mutual relations. As for Genkaku, whenever he had a little leisure, he would sit in his hut, read the sutras and practice seated meditation. This he would do every day.

Well then, one day, having heard rumors about him, a yamabushi from some other place came along and peeked in at his hut.

"Hey, Genkaku, it seems as though you're doing quite well," the man said, walking right into Genkaku's hut. "Are you satisfied with that?" he continued. "It's unfortunate that you're not making more money. How about it? Pair up with me and we'll make a good profit."

Genkaku heard this but continued chanting his sutras and did not even turn around. Then he rebuked the man "I don't know who you are or where you came from, but I'm not joining in talk of such evil schemes. Go away!"

"Humph," the man replied. "I'm a yamabushi just like you. You're looking down at me because I'm dressed in tatters."

"I still haven't taken a look at you," Genkaku answered. "But what you're saying goes against the Way of Man. So I cannot count you as one of us yamabushi." At this response, the "yamabushi" departed.

Not but a few days after this, fires continually broke out in village after village.

"What's going on?"

"Huh! A troublemaker must be going around at night . . ."

"We must be vigilant and appoint a night watchman."

"Who could be the culprit?"

Such talk was circulating around the area and people were being driven mad.

While this anger was being spewed forth, a priest's ceremonial conch shell was discovered at the site of one of the burned houses.

"What! Genkaku . . . Genkaku!" And immediately the criminal was taken to be Genkaku.

"But why would Genkaku-sama do such a terrible thing?" someone asked.

"You can't judge a man by his appearance!" was the response, and one night the villagers could contain themselves no longer. Holding torches to light the way, and armed with hoes and sickles, they pushed their way up to the hut on the pass and set fire to it. From inside the hut that was in flames, Genkaku's voice echoed as he chanted a sutra.

"Genkaku! Genkaku!" the people called as they waited for the yamabushi they supposed would come running out at any time. But the sound of the sutra did not stop and, as it continued, the flames grew stronger until the house collapsed. And there in the smoldering ruins they found Genkaku's remains.

"That swine!" they yelled, and kicked the remains about with their feet. With this, the people calmed down and returned down the pass with sighs of relief.

After that, the fires that had been breaking out in the local villages ceased and people nodded to themselves that, after all, the miscreant must have been Genkaku. But not long after this, pale fireballs flew through the sky almost every night, sending fear deep into their breasts. Then during the day fireballs appeared from the bottom of the pass and rose up to darken the sun. The people were so frightened that they could no longer settle down to their work. As they trembled in fear wondering what this could be, the fires began again, more frequently than before.

The miscreant was caught not long after that. It was a yam-abushi that seemed to be drinking sake all day long, soliciting food to eat and, when refused, setting houses on fire out of spite. This was the yamabushi who had called in on Genkaku, but of course this was not known to anyone other than Gen-kaku, whom the villagers had killed.

But now the people finally realized that the arsonist was not Genkaku.

"Ahh, Genkaku-sama, we have truly done something evil," they lamented. "Please forgive us." The villagers went up to the pass and prostrated themselves on the ground in apology. But this was not all. They erected a grave mound at the site of the hut at the Aruga Pass and held a service for him there.

From that time on, the fireballs no longer appeared, but people's mistakes can be frightening, can't they?

The Buddha Who Lived among Us

Ryodo was the resident priest at a temple in Matsushiro, and hated to kill living things from the time he was young.

He was raised in the town of Nagano, and one day in his childhood, when he was tilling a rice field, he saw blood flowing from an earthworm that had been cut in half by his hoe.

"Ahh, I killed it," he thought. Understanding that he had taken a life with his own hands, Ryodo sadly returned to his home and announced that he would no longer go out to work in the rice fields.

So it was decided that he would be apprenticed to the shop of a merchant, and soon he was put in the charge of a clog-maker. At the clog shop, they cut up paulownia wood, made clogs from that and sold them. But Ryodo was concerned about the way the shop did business. One paulownia tree, ten sen; cutting that up in pieces and making clogs would be twenty or thirty sen charged to a customer . . . this made him feel uneasy.

So in the end, he slipped away from the shop without telling anyone and, setting his eyes in the direction of Mount Togakushi, began climbing.

This threw his unknowing family and the clog maker into great confusion.

When he got as far as the rocky peak of Mount Iizuna, he began to practice seated meditation. Declaring that he wanted to become like the Buddha, Lord Shaka, he chanted the Nembutsu.

Ryodo became a resident priest after all this. In his head, he thought that killing even the smallest living being was unforgivable, he was careful as he walked about not to kill a single ant; and if he did, he would always chant Namu Amida Butsu. He would not even kill the lice that crowded on his body and was patient even when they crawled over his back and stomach.

But one night, the master of a house where he had stayed over, asked, "Ryodo, were you unable to sleep last night? You went out into the garden a number of times."

"Yes," he answered. "Lice were getting all over me, so each time, I went out to the garden to let them loose."

◊   ◊   ◊

To be sure, Ryodo was a friend of the weak and for this reason, he was a friend of the poor as well. When begging for alms, he had noticed that he would receive nothing from the houses of the wealthy. He did, however, receive alms from the homes of the poor.

"Why is this?" he was asked.

"The wealthy do not understand the value of things," he always answered. "But the poor understand this well. The Buddha will not rejoice when receiving something from those who do not understand this value. People must have hearts as broad as the sea."

Ryodo pulled along a cart with pots and kettles and a load of rice, and a banner on which Namu Amida Butsu was written, and was accompanied by old folk and even children as he led them to see the beautiful sea at Naoetsu.

Those who admired Ryodo called him a "present-day Shaka." In the end, he sent out postcards to all of them, saying that he would be going to paradise on the eighth day of the eleventh month, and he passed away true to that prediction. This was in 1921.

Loincloth Ichibei

Ichibei lived in a small hut on a hill just outside his village. The villagers regarded him as a strange person and liked to make fun of him.

During the summer of one particular year, no rain fell and the heat continued day after day. "The way it's going, the rice fields are going to dry up," the villagers lamented, going around with sad expressions.

It was finally determined that they would have to hold a prayer for rain, and both the old folks and the children gathered at the shrine all together and made a great commotion, praying and striking bells. They respectfully tied sacred paper strips to the pillars of a raised platform inside the temple.

However, no rain fell at all.

Well then, as the villagers prayed and chanted, Ichibei, wearing only a loincloth, was sleeping and snoring in his hut, but suddenly jumped up.

"What's this?" he muttered. "A prayer for rain?" And he left for the village shrine.

Everyone looked at him with eyes that said, "The strange one has come again!"

But at this, Ichibei abruptly unfastened his loincloth, leapt onto the platform, and fastened the loincloth to the pillar alongside the sacred paper strips. Shouting, "Ha, ha! Oh ho!" he started to dance.

People yelled that he had gone crazy and that someone should stop him, but just then Ichibei grabbed a drum from a man and danced as he beat it—*te ten, te ten*!

Yet, just as people grimaced at what an embarrassment he was, the sky clouded over and rain fell in buckets.

"Ahh! Rain! Rain!"

"What a blessing!"

And everyone greatly rejoiced.

That year, the harvests were plentiful and the people were relieved beyond measure. And the way people viewed Ichibei also changed.

"This was thanks to Ichibei," they said to each other, expressing their gratitude.

That autumn, there was so much rice, so many potatoes and so many daikon radishes delivered to Ichibei's hut that he would never lack for things to eat.

The Wealthy Charcoal Maker

Long ago in the capital, there was a young princess called Amano-hime. She was born into the house of a court official but was not what you would call attractive and reached her eighteenth year without any prospects of being married.

Princess Amano-hime and her mother were both worried and went to pray at the Sumiyoshi Shrine for ten days and ten nights. The shrine god then manifested itself and said, "Your mate will be Kitoji, a charcoal maker who lives in Sonohara in the province of Shinano. It is a long journey, but you should go now."

"What? Shinano?"

Princess Amano-hime had no idea what kind of a journey this would be, but went together with two companions. Asking people on the road again and again, they finally found their way to Sonohara.

"Princess Amano-hime, you must be thirsty," said one of her companions, and handed her a bowl of water.

"Ahh, what delicious water . . . and what beautiful scenery," Princess Amano-hime exclaimed.

Just at that time, a man was coming down the mountain, and Princess Amano-hime's companion asked, "May I inquire if you know of a man in this place by the name of Kitoji?"

The man stared at her vacantly and replied, "Kitoji? That would be me."

"Kitoji the charcoal maker?"

"Yes, that's right."

Hearing this, Princess Amano-hime looked surprised and asked the man his name again just to make sure. Nevertheless, when she understood that this very plain man was very much the one spoken of by the god of the Sumiyoshi Shrine, tears filled her eyes.

"Why is this so distressing?" Kitoji asked?

"No, no," Princess Amano-hime said, trying to repair the situation. "I'm so happy to have met you . . ."

"You mean you've taken a fancy to me?" Kitoji laughed.

In the end, Princess Amano-hime was taken by the man's simplicity and, thinking again of her own plain appearance, explained to him truthfully everything that had occurred up until now. Hearing all this, it was Kitoji's turn to be surprised.

"That is such a welcome story, but it's more than I deserve to have such a high-class woman as my wife," he said quite abashed. But in the end, they did become husband and wife.

Kitoji's charcoal-making shop was just a little structure of thatch, while inside was just a single small iron pot. Quite naturally, Princess Amano-hime took a gloomy view of this little hut and felt that now the time had come, she would change things for the better. Taking out a clump of gold she had received from her father, she asked Kitoji to go into to town and use it to buy some rice, salt and fish.

Kitoji took the gold and, gazing upon it, went out. He knew nothing about the value of the metal and, while playing with it in his hand, went along the bank of the Achi River on his way into town. But he hadn't gone very far when he stopped and exclaimed, "Oh! The cranes have come again."

In an area of standing water, two cranes were flapping their wings. Kitoji had tried and failed to catch he birds previously. "Now!" he thought, and quickly threw the gold he carried at them. He failed to hit them however, and the gold clump sank into the river with a splash. Up in the sky, the cranes honked as though they were making fun of him.

Kitoji stood there and thought for a moment, "Now what was it that I came out here for . . . ? Ah, yes. She said I was to take that into town and do this and that." He remembered Princess Amano-hime's words, but since he no longer had the metal clump she had given him, he returned to their hut.

"What's this?" Princess Amano-hime greeted him. "Is the town so close by?"

"No, um, uh . . ." and Kitoji told her what had happened.

She was astonished at this and sobbed convulsively, explaining that gold was something very valuable that could rarely be come by.

"Oh? Is that right?" Kitoji replied. "If that's so, we can go to that little branch of the Sumiyoshi Shrine at the mountain right behind the town and get as much as we want."

And this time, it was Princess Amano-hime's turn to be surprised.

"Really?"

"Yes. Let's go take a look." And with this the two climbed the mountain, and behind the shrine was a mountain of gold.

"When I was burning charcoal, I offered the best pieces to the god of Sumiyoshi," he explained.

Princess Amano-hime was deeply moved by his faith. She understood that this was the divine guidance of the god of Sumiyoshi, and felt great respect for Kitoji.

After that, the two worked with hearts together, in the end were respected by everyone, and became so rich that Kitoji became known as the "Wealthy Charcoal Maker."

His fame eventually reached the capital, and Princess Amano-hime's parents were said to be overjoyed.

The Woman Who Could Not Tell Her Name

It was a terrible period when women could not speak their names even though they were doing important work.

Long ago, a place called Unnodaira was broad and fertile enough to raise crops, but often, there were long periods of drought. When their crops were drying up, the people were agitated. Although they complained, there was no one who could combine knowhow and effort to be able to help.

Then, one summer, just as farmers were lamenting once more about the inevitable drought, a large woman with long disheveled hair appeared and exclaimed to the villagers, "Why are you grieving without taking action? Listen to what I'm going to say!"

"Who are you?"

"What can a woman do?"

"Stop acting like a fool."

Although they yelled at her as if she was a half-wit, the woman calmly spoke to those who had gathered around her.

"The fact that you have insufficient water has arisen from your complete reliance on the gods of Heaven. Don't you know that the gods have good moods and bad?"

Everyone stood silently, wondering if the woman was a messenger from the gods.

"You are neglecting what you yourselves can do, and are finding no solution," the woman said. "The gods bringing a halt to the rain is also a warning for you to use your own intelligence. Do some construction to make a channel to draw water from the Kan River over there. Everyone bring your hoes and plows, and put some effort into it!" And thus she urged them on.

But some complained that there were not enough people for that.

"If there are not enough here," she went on, "there are plenty of people in this world. So go out and employ some."

With relieved looks on their faces, the people were struck by the woman's counsel. Convinced by her words, they did what the woman said, and hurried out with her to gather some workers and, very quickly, the work advanced. The woman pointed out exactly where the channel should be dug, the villagers ran back and forth every day in accordance with her instructions, and finally the channel was finished.

In this way, even when there were times when no rain fell at all, the farmers of Unnodaira were able to work hard at their crops.

It is a great shame that the woman's name and where she came from are not spoken of, to this day.

The Legend of Shinzaburo

Shinzaburo was a hunter, famous for his ability with a gun, and every day before leaving his house to go to the mountain, he would polish his firearm.

Now he saw that the more he polished his gun, the more skillful he became, and one day, when he encountered a Tengu goblin, he shot down the fan it was carrying and returned home full of pride.

"Listen," he boasted, "I went over to the forest at the lake and a pine tree was shaking rather strangely. By chance, I took a look, and there was a Tengu laughing at me. It was a Tengu with big ears. When I asked it what was so funny, it said that my skill at shooting wasn't much, and that the monkeys were making fun of me. Then I got angry."

According to Shinzaburo's story, he took aim and shot once. But the Tengu flew casually to the top of a cedar tree flapping its fan and said, "How about it? Try to shoot this." Shinzaburo immediately let fly again and somehow the fan was split right in two and fell to the ground.

Everyone in the village praised him for his skill, but Shinzaburo laughed in an embarrassed manner, showing himself as just a good-natured person.

Some days later he went again to the lake and heard a noise—*pachin pachin*—coming from a stone hut on a cliff. With his rifle in one hand, he peeked in through the entranceway. And there was the big-eared Tengu from the other day playing a game of Go with another Tengu he had never seen before.

"Huh. Relaxing at Go?" thought Shinzaburo to himself, and went inside.

"You shoot a gun," the big-eared Tengu said. "But can you play Go?"

"Um ... er ... yes ... ," Shinzaburo answered vaguely, for he was not very good at all.

"Well then, if that's so, I'll have a bout with you, seeing as you won our first encounter," he laughed.

Had he fled at this point, Shinzaburo's vanity would have been wounded, even though he had shown himself to be a good shot; and so he sat himself down.

The two Tengu continued playing Go with a *pachin pachin* as though enjoying themselves, but the game did not come to an end.

In the meanwhile, Shinzaburo became sleepy and, holding his rifle upright in one hand, dozed off. Nonetheless, he kept one eye open and waited for the game to finish.

"If I run away, they'll make fun of me," was all that was in his head. And with that in mind, there was no reason to leave while the game the Tengu were playing continued.

"Extraordinary," Shinzaburo mumbled. "This bout seems never to end."

"For Tengu, the game of Go goes beyond time," the big-eared Tengu said. "So someone like you, a human being that lives a narrow life, gets impatient I suppose."

"Hmm ..." Shinzaburo did not understand, and in the middle of his response, fell asleep again.

After a long while when he opened his eyes again, he noticed that it had grown dark outside. But the Tengu were still playing Go, and Shinzaburo, though quite brave himself, was worried about those at home.

"I'm getting hungry," he said. "I'm going home to eat, then I'll be back." And so saying, he went outside. But when he arrived at his gate there was a crowd of people stirring about.

"Huh?" he thought as he heard a priest chanting a sutra.

"What's this," he yelled as he hurried into the house. "Did my mother die? What's happened?"

His wife jumped up and greeted him with a shocked voice.

"Whose memorial service is this?" he asked.

"What are you saying?" asked the priest. "It's for you, Shinzaburo," he said, which totally shocked him.

"You went out hunting and didn't come back for years," his wife said, laughing through her tears. "We thought you had died and had a funeral for you seven years ago. So this is the seventh year anniversary ceremony."

"Huh! What a strange story," Shinzaburo said, cocking his head to the side. "I went out to the lake and there were some Tengu playing Go. I just watched them and came back."

His wife thereupon took his gun from him and held it in her hand. "Look how rusty it is. It's absolutely red, isn't it?" she said, and she showed him the corroded gun, where even the wooden parts had become ragged.

"Well, I'll be damned," he muttered to himself. "That Tengu got its revenge."

And looking as though he had awakened from a dream, he stood there biting his lip.

The Carp Princess

Long ago, the Azusa River, which flowed down from the Hida mountain range caused alarm when continuing daily rains made the river swell, threatening to destroy the levees.

In the village of Hata, there at the upper reaches of the river, the people built lookout huts along the levee and would take turns to monitor the situation every day and every night.

There was a young, easygoing man by the name of Genkichi who lived in the village. One night, after three days of rain that was showing no sign of stopping, this Genkichi, along with three others, was appointed to be at a lookout hut.

"Well, you go ahead and sleep, I'll keep watch by myself," he said to the others. He put on a straw raincoat and, swinging a paper lantern, went out to walk along the bank of the levee. Now it was a very serious thing if just a little water leaked through, as the village could be washed away in an instant.

Genkichi advanced downstream, checking for leaks in the levee with his hands. Up ahead he saw a faint ring of light and in the center of that light was the figure of a person. Thinking that this was maybe a dream, he rubbed his eyes and moved closer. As he did this, the figure in the center of the light—a woman in a kimono holding an umbrella—quickly walked away in the opposite direction. Looking carefully, it seemed that she was wearing clogs with red thongs, and her footsteps sent her slipping lightly along on top of the levee.

"This is certainly a Kitsune fox demon or a Tanuki raccoon-dog yokai," he thought suspiciously as he advanced. Then, from behind her, he said, "Excuse me . . ."

In that instant she turned around with a face inexpressibly beautiful. Genkichi was attracted to her on the spot, and his heart started pounding. "What are you doing here on a night like this?" he asked casually.

"I came to look at the water," she said smilingly with a voice like the tinkling of a bell. Whether it was the way she spoke or her gestures, she was a woman you would not see in this part of the country.

"Yes, but in such a pretty kimono?" he asked.

"Please don't ask me about that," she answered. "I just want to return to my village quickly, and I can't go back looking shabby."

Genkichi was puzzled and could say nothing.

"You seem to have taken a liking to me," she continued. "And for me, I like an easygoing man like you."

"Y-yes . . . ," Genkichi stammered. "So would you meet me again tomorrow night?"

Hearing this, the woman looked sad and shook her head and said that that was not her decision.

"What does that mean?" Genkichi asked.

"I am an bad woman who wants to flood the river and wash away the town and its fields," she replied. "I myself do not understand why, but since we have sworn our love together, this would go against our nature."

"What does 'our' mean?" he asked.

"I cannot say that on my own," she said.

And with this, the woman and the ring of light disappeared without a sound, right before Genkichi's eyes.

Genkichi returned to the hut but did not tell anyone about meeting the beautiful woman. He kept it to himself because he hoped to meet her again.

◊   ◊   ◊

The next night, Genkichi went out again to the hut by himself. As he walked along the path on the levee, he thought about the mysterious woman and the meaning of her words of the night before and waited for her to appear.

"Hmm," he thought, "If I hide myself and wait, I should be able to know her true form." And he hid himself in the thicket below the levee and crouched down on his heels. The rain continued to fall—no change from the day before. He wondered where the woman's village might be and thought of what she had said about flooding the river and other things—it was all full of riddles.

After a while, he thought he heard the sound of the clogs, and again he saw the faint light up ahead. Then, the woman dressed in a kimono and holding an umbrella was walking quietly along the top of the levee, coming his way.

The woman was so beautiful, Genkichi was tempted to meet and talk with her again, but controlled himself and continued to watch. The woman looked up, pointed at the sky with the tip of her umbrella and said with a limpid voice, "More rain. More rain, please."

She then fixed her eyes on the river, and made a strange request: "Tomorrow, carry me to my village."

After that, the woman returned toward the village in the direction from which she had come. Wondering where she was going, Genkichi followed along behind her until she came to the large Ota mansion. The woman then disappeared through the gate.

The Ota mansion was famous for being the grandest house in the village. It had a large garden with a pond. But other than the master of the house, his elderly mother and some servants, there was no woman of such beauty there.

This riddle now deepened for Genkichi, and he returned to the hut and spoke to his two companions about everything that had happened up to then.

"So perhaps tomorrow we should go to the mansion and tell the master about this."

"But this is maybe a secret that shouldn't be disclosed."

The three men were at a loss of what to do. Not only was there the imminent danger of the river flooding, but there was the problem of what they should or shouldn't say.

But the following day, the three men set off for the Ota mansion and told the story straightforwardly.

"Ah, of course," the master exclaimed. "There's no mistaking—it's the fish known as the Carp Princess we have in our pond. The legend is that in about her thousandth year, the Carp Princess calls down a heavy rain and returns to the place where she was born in the Azusa River. Now this must be that thousandth year, and the carp's intention must be to call the water of the river into the pond and to return to her hometown carried by the floodwaters."

"Aha, could that be it?" Genkichi exclaimed in surprise. It certainly fit with the woman's strange request about being carried to her village and was a reasonable explanation.

"If I had not heard this story," the master said gratefully, "the village would have been flooded and washed away. Although the Carp Princess may not be carried away to her hometown, there must be other methods of getting her there."

"Yes," one of the young men said. "Let's carry her down on a shutter or something."

Agreements were reached that very day, and on the following day it was arranged to carry away the Carp Princess. The men who were to carry her were informed, many people gathered at the Ota mansion and all were treated to sake. As they were drinking, the sky cleared and the gloom vanished. A six-foot-long carp was set on a large rain shutter and, on the shoulders of Genkichi and his fellows, went out of the gate.

There is no need to mention the villagers' joy at not being flooded. Genkichi, however, returned home, never took the job of night lookout again, and dreamed of that beautiful princess for a long, long time.

PART 13

STORIES FROM THE SAMURAI ERA

The Acolyte Who Turned into a Ghost

The training involved in serving the Buddha includes a good number of trying activities. Those charged with the upkeep of the temple, no matter how young, must live their lives day by day following the instructions of the priest. The best of priests will have a good understanding of how to discipline young monks and will conceal a gentleness inside of strict instruction. But there have also been priests of an abusive nature.

It seems that such a priest was living in a temple in the village of Hotaka, and there is a story about a twelve-year-old child from a neighboring village who was entrusted to be trained as a practitioner of Buddhist austerities, and how this ended in failure. And rather than call this child a practitioner of Buddhist austerities, an acolyte would be a better word.

One day the priest called the acolyte and said, "Listen, it's been a month since you came here. I've been watching you up until now and it seems that your weak point is fear of the dark of night. But with that kind of cowardice, you'll never become a priest. All right? From tonight you're going to do as I say."

"Yes," the upset acolyte simply replied, without moving from the seated position he had taken before the priest.

"There is a small shrine beyond the temple," the priest continued, "and it's been my duty to set up the candles there for a long time. But from tonight, I'll have you carry out that task, do you understand?"

The acolyte turned completely pale. "Please . . . please spare me just that. I'll do anything else."

That the acolyte had turned pale was not without reason. To reach this shrine, one had to walk quickly through a graveyard and a cedar forest that was dark even during the day. It was beneath these large cedar trees that the shrine was kept. Setting up the candles, however, was to be done at two o'clock in the morning.

"Please spare me this," the acolyte cried, touching his head to the floor.

But the priest looked down on him coldly and said, "You fool! What are you going to do with such a weak spirit? What a coward! From tonight on, you'll do as I said. Do you understand? If not, I won't forgive you!"

Seeing that the priest was not going to retreat even a single step, the acolyte promised that he would do as he'd been told.

That night at two o'clock, the acolyte took the candles in trembling hands and walked through the cedar forest with the aid of a paper lantern. But now he could hear the cries of an owl in the dark night, and now what seemed to be the approach of foxes or wolves, and he felt so afraid that his knees started to tremble. He got to a point where he could not take one step further, and instead, he panicked and ran back to the temple. But there was the priest, standing there just waiting for him.

"What's this? For shame! I was watching you!" And with that, he took a long staff that he was carrying and beat the acolyte mercilessly on his buttocks and back.

The acolyte cried and shrieked that he would go and, pulling himself together, somehow completed his duty that night.

◊   ◊   ◊

Three nights later, as the acolyte was resting in his room, the priest came inside. "Last night," he said, "you took advantage of my absence and didn't go as you were supposed to," and once again mercilessly beat the boy with his staff.

The acolyte apologized, saying that he was tired out from chopping firewood and had overslept. The priest, however, would hear none of his excuses and beat him all the more.

On the fifth night, an unusually strong autumn wind was blowing and not a star appeared in the sky. The acolyte, however, was fearful of being beaten with the staff, and there was nothing else to be done, so he lit a paper lantern and proceeded through the howling cedar forest. But the wind blew the lantern away and very quickly all was completely dark. The boy let out a scream and began running desperately back to the temple. But just at that moment, a voice rang out, and someone grabbed him by the neck.

There was no mistaking; it was the priest.

"I thought you would be just like this," the priest said. "Well, there's no forgiving you now. Come along!"

The priest jerked the acolyte along to the shrine and tied him to a tree there with a rope he had been carrying. The boy begged for forgiveness, but the priest just told him to reflect upon himself until morning, lit the candles in the shrine himself and left. Nothing then remained but the sound of the weeping acolyte.

"What an annoying creature," the priest mumbled as he returned to the temple. "If this doesn't work, there's nothing more I can do but drive him away." And he waited for the dawn. Then, having finished his breakfast, the priest heaved a sigh of exasperation and entered the cedar forest. He made his way to the tree where he had tied the acolyte.

"Well, how about it?" he sneered. "Have you thought this matter over?" He grabbed the boy by the hand, then suddenly gasped. The acolyte hung there limp, with his eyes closed.

The priest shouted and shook the boy's shoulders, but the acolyte's face had turned white and his lips had become dark. Totally shaken, the priest grasped the boy's wrist and checked his pulse.

He was dead.

His heart pounding, the priest untied the rope, hid the corpse in a thicket and ran back to the temple. Carrying a mattock and keeping a sharp lookout, he dug a hole beneath a cedar tree and buried the body.

"It's better that nobody knows," he thought.

The priest passed an unsettled day, and in the middle of the night went out to light the candles at the shrine. As he began this rite, a white light floated vaguely in the tops of the cedar trees and came down unsteadily in the direction of the priest, who started shaking all over and then fled.

"A gh . . . ghost! It's the acolyte's ghost," he stammered as he ran.

After this, the temple was abandoned. A pale white fireball would sometimes appear in its vicinity, and this would terrify the villagers.

Nobody knew the truth but the priest, so perhaps he disclosed the story at some point from a bad conscience, and it may have been passed down in this way.

Kumahachi's Defeat of the Ghost

"What? There's a ghost at that temple?"

Kumahachi heard this rumor at his hut in a rocky place in the mountains, where he was feeling depressed at having failed to catch a Daija snake. He was famed for his ability with a gun, having once shot down eight bears in a single day. Thinking that if a ghost must be shot, it should be left to him, he went down from the highlands of Sugadaira to the village of Suzaka, where they talked of nothing but the ghost.

The ghost was said to be an Oni demon with bones sticking out from a sea-snail-shaped head. Every night it would appear at the large temple in the village and snatch people up, scattering their bones beneath the temple's main gate.

Kumahachi listened to all of the villagers' stories, then one pleasant moonlit night, shouldered his gun and hid in the shadow of the main gate. Suddenly he felt a warm breeze beginning to waft through and then, from the temple grounds, there came a groan like nothing he had ever heard before. The groan spread through a large zelkova tree in the garden and gradually came in the direction of the gate. The ghost's form could not be seen.

"That's it!" Kumahachi thought, and tightened his resolve.

Then, a dark black shadow came obliquely from the main gate and crossed in Kumahachi's direction. Kumahachi instantly fired a shot. There was the sound of having hit his mark, and at that moment he could feel something dripping onto him. A black cloud whirled up into the sky with a scream and flew off to the east.

When the morning light began to dawn, Kumahachi saw that his body was stained with blood. Thinking that the creature could no longer be alive, he returned to his mountain hut, telling no one that he had quelled the ghost.

◊   ◊   ◊

Several decades later, a ginkgo tree withered away completely at the Fuganji Temple, over in the east at the foot of Mount Bozu. The priest thought this was strange, reasoning that ginkgo trees rarely withered and died. Calling the villagers together, he had them cut the roots of the tree and take a look. When this was done, a hole broke open at the root.

The priest and the others there cocked their heads in surprise at this, and when one of them peeped into the hole, he cried out in fear and fell back.

When they all gazed into the hole, they saw the remains of a skull with bones and teeth protruding from it. More surprising was a hole in the skull, which held something that looked like a bullet.

The people talked this over amongst themselves, thinking that this must have been the ghost that had caused so much havoc over at the village some time ago, but could not make sense of the bullet. Kumahachi's name never came up.

Kumahachi was not a man with self-pride and, as was his wont, never spoke to anyone about subduing the Oni. He was at this time passing his days lying sick in bed. The people around him spoke about the skull being discovered at the village, then buried with the priest chanting the Nembutsu; and about the bullet hitting the Oni's forehead, and what a man it must have been who shot it. But while such talk would have reached his ears, Kumahachi only responded with a "Really? Is that so?" and finally breathed his last.

The Ghost Bean

Long ago, in a place called Kuisege, there was an old lady who was both ill-natured and a liar. The villagers agreed that they had never encountered such obstinacy and talked of how they couldn't wait for her to die. When such talk reached the old lady's ears, she would mutter, "What fools! I'm not going to die any time soon."

But one night, a little Ko-oni demon appeared at her pillow in a dream.

"I'm a retainer of Enma, the King of Hell," the Ko-oni explained, "and he has sent me here as a messenger. The fact is that Hell is currently full, and Enma says that he's so busy that he's exhausted. He is unable to receive even an ill-tempered old lady like you right now, but I'll come back for you in a hundred days."

In the morning, the old lady thought over her dream of the night before. "Huh!" she reflected. "Another fool. Doesn't he know that I'm in the best of health? There's no way I'm about to die."

And she was as ill-tempered as ever.

But as the days passed by, somehow her body would not move as she wanted and in addition she became emaciated and pale.

So even this obstinate old lady became uneasy and went to visit the priest at the Shotokuji Temple. "I don't want to die yet," she cried, explaining the situation to the priest. "What can I do?"

"Well, that's a shame," the priest said to her bluntly. "But you know, our predestined span of life is not something we can change."

"Then, at least how can I keep myself from falling into Hell?" she implored.

The priest then counseled her that the only way that she could avoid such a fate was to chant the Nembutsu every day and to rely on the Buddha.

Hearing this, the old lady became meek and gentle, and sat before the Buddhist altar every day. But then, the Ko-oni appeared to her once again in a dream.

"Well, haven't you been chanting the Nembutsu every day? We can't take a person such as you into Hell, and Enma is quite angry," it declared and quickly disappeared.

The old lady realized that she was not going to fall into Hell and was overjoyed. Knowing that this was thanks to the priest, she put some beans that she had just picked from her garden into a tiered box, tied it up in a kerchief and was about to take it to the temple. But just at that moment, her mind grew dark and she collapsed and died.

In the same hour, however, she appeared at the main hall of the Shotokuji Temple, where the priest was chanting a sutra.

"Ahh, honorable priest," she said. "I'm so happy. Last night a messenger from Enma came, and told me that I will not be falling into Hell." And she held out the box of beans she had carried, explaining that they were from her own garden and for him to eat.

The priest thanked her and placed the box before the Buddhist altar. He then invited the old lady into an interior room, offering her tea and cakes. But the old lady did not drink the tea or touch the cakes. She sat there silently, and as the priest watched in horror, she slowly started to disappear.

The priest was astonished, but just then an old man who lived next to the old lady ran up and informed him that she had passed away.

"What?" And the priest explained that he had just been talking to her right there.

When the old man assured him that she had died, the priest was shaken and went outside. He then went to her house to see her collapsed corpse himself, and there, next to her body was a tiered box of beans. All the more surprised, the priest finally realized that the old lady who had come to the temple was a ghost.

After that, the villagers called those beans "ghost beans," and when they planted them, they always bore a rich crop.

The Hot Spring That Ran with Blood

This is a story about the time when the samurai were still arrogant and proud. Even when the period of wars was over, the samurai still held their heads high and were strongly against marrying their daughters to farmers or merchants.

Nevertheless, tender passion will transcend social position and give birth to a relationship of loving and being loved.

Well then, one day, a samurai went incognito to the hot spring at Yamabe, and, accompanied by his daughter, stayed at an inn there for a number of days. The young men who lived near the inn talked widely among themselves, remarking on the young woman's beauty, demanding to be the first to have a claim on her, and she became the target of longing among those men.

During that time, the young girl secretly fell in love with a poor young charcoal maker in the area, and their feelings were mutual. Her father then heard of this and was bitterly troubled. If this was true, he thought, he would not be able to show his face to his fellow samurai.

He was now placed in the critical and pathetic position of either taking a stand or acquiescing to his daughter, and this made him tremble with anger.

Ordinarily, he should have confronted his daughter and tell her that he heard that she had recently been meeting with a poor man of a different social class, and that this was unacceptable. But this samurai was a coward and instead took a roundabout way.

"You have a reputation as a young lady from a good family," he counseled her. "I am waiting for the future when you can meet a good man—a samurai with an excellent character. So please do nothing untoward."

The young lady, however, did not understand her father's

feelings and, late at night, avoiding her parent's eyes, she would slip outside. But on one such a night, her father had the feeling that she had silently left her room and went to check. Finding that she had gone, he set off in search of her, muttering to himself, sword in hand.

It was a beautiful starry night and he could see her silhouette passing through the forest and going down in the direction of the mountain stream. He continued to follow her and at last, coming to the bank of the stream, he saw the outline of a young man.

"Ahh, have you really come?" the young man said when he saw the samurai's daughter, embracing her. "I thought that you would not be coming back again."

"I'm so sorry," she exclaimed. "My father . . . my father seems to suspect us, so I stole out of the inn."

"It's all right," the young man replied. "No matter what happens, I love you and will always love you."

"Yes, and I love you," she returned. "If the worst happens, I'll be with you wherever you go."

Now her father, who had concealed himself in a thicket, had taken this in and was boiling over in anger. Suddenly he leapt out unsheathing his sword and cut through his daughter's back with a single stroke.

The girl screamed, fell to the ground and died.

"Forgive me," her father cried, his eyes bright with tears.

The young man, who had not understood this turn of events, stared vacantly at the assailant and then drew up to him. Recognizing him as the girl's father, he cried out, fell to the ground and clung to his lover.

"The girl took liberty with her status," the man said. "I simply followed the Way of the Samurai."

And with that, he climbed silently up the bank and disappeared beneath the stars that now seemed to be falling from the sky.

Overcome with grief, the young man returned to his hut.

Then, mumbling, "What is status . . . status . . . status . . ." over and over, with tears flooding his eyes and going crazy with anger, he leapt into the burning coal kiln and followed after his lover.

After that, the smell of death drifted from the chimney at the Yamabe hot spring and the baths were stained with bright red blood.

The Bride-Killing Field

Long ago, there was an ill-tempered old lady. Her husband had died early on and her son had married a young woman, but he, too, had passed away.

The old lady blamed the young wife for all of her own unhappiness and criticized her for everything she did. Every time she ate a meal, she would say, "When a bride comes, she does not eat sitting on the tatami matting. She should eat on the wooden floor of the kitchen," then turn her back on her and sit on the tatami. She would even throw her rice bowl across the room, saying that she couldn't eat such stuff. The gentle wife would apologize every day and bow her head to the floor.

Then one day . . .

"Well, planting season starts tomorrow—I'm going to bed," the old lady said, and went quickly to sleep. Throughout the night, the young wife had a headache, the baby was crying, she was unable to sleep well and when the morning came, she was feeling drowsy. Nevertheless, she did not complain about her poor condition and, putting together her preparations, went out to the rice paddies with her mother-in-law. Then, carrying her baby on her back, she put all her energies into planting the rice.

Her mother-in-law was in the habit of sitting down and resting on the ridges between the paddies when she got tired, while not giving the wife time to even breastfeed the baby. The wife continued to work, shedding tears.

"Ahh, my hips hurt so much," the old lady complained, and as the planting of the seedlings went on, the sun began to go down. "Well, I'm going home," she continued. "You stay here by yourself. But don't come back until you finish, even when it gets dark. You'll cause us embarrassment throughout the neighborhood. If you come back before finishing, I'll not let you eat dinner." And, washing the mud of the rice paddy from her feet, she left immediately.

"But . . ." the wife cried plaintively. The old lady did not even turn around to look. The wife was overcome with sorrow. Moreover, half of the paddy had still not been planted with seedlings. No matter how hard she worked, it was clear that she would not be able to finish by the time the sun set. The baby on her back was crying from hunger, her own head was becoming dim and everything was turning black before her eyes.

Even so, she continued with the rice-planting as though in prayer. Was the sun starting to set earlier than usual that day? She wasn't sure.

"By the time the sun sinks . . . by the time the sun sinks . . ."

With her heart beating fast, the young wife checked the position of the sun from time to time and continued on. But the sun kept on sinking without pity and she couldn't stop herself from crying. Finally, there was no way she could finish the planting by sunset.

The baby let out a cry, and just at that moment, the sun went down behind the mountains.

"Ahh, please, please Lord Sun, come up just one more time," the woman prayed through her tears. And the sun, which should have become hidden now, suddenly leapt up over the mountains. But just as she expressed her joy, she was aware that something had fallen down behind her, and when she looked, her baby's head was rolling along the ground.

When she understood what had happened, the young wife collapsed head first into a channel of water and died.

The Master of a Sad Deception

Long ago in a certain village, there was a young man by the name of Moshichi who was popularly known for his ability to mimic the cries of cats, the grunts of pigs and the voices of other people. As a sort of side show during festivals he was much in demand and was well paid to boot.

As a result of this, Moshichi gradually stopped working in the fields and passed his days idly.

However, there came a time when both of his parents fell ill and died. A neighbor by the name of Nizaemon was unable to let this pass unnoticed. Remembering that Moshichi had loved horses when he was young, he put him to work with his own horse.

This was indeed a difficult time for Moshichi, so he gratefully moved to Nizaemon's house and, uncharacteristically, began to work hard.

Every morning before breakfast, he would lead the horse out of the stable, cut hay in the mountain over two miles away and return with six bundles of hay on the horse's back and four bundles on his own. As soon as he arrived at the house, he would feed the horse and ladle water for it to drink. Only then would he eat his own breakfast.

Nizaemon watched this and expressed his admiration to his wife. Moshichi never looked askance at working in the rice paddies either and always finished his work there. The more Moshichi was praised, the harder the young man worked, but as the year went on, autumn and its festivals came around again.

"Wait a minute," Moshichi thought to himself. "Certainly I've received money from my employer, but compared to the rewards I received from being a mimic, not much."

And after coming to this conclusion, he suddenly started

acting foolishly. At the same time, he gradually began slacking at his work and feeling nostalgia for the time when he was a mimic.

One day, just when Moshichi was in the stable giving a bucket of water to the horse, a cat came up and started meowing noisily and following him about. Then, as he was chasing the cat, he expertly imitated its cries himself, and the cat ran off toward the kitchen. But even then, Moshichi went on imitating its cries.

"Huh!" Nizaemon's wife said from the kitchen. "The cat is right here, so what can this be?"

Hearing this, a wicked idea immediately floated up in Moshichi's mind. "Why didn't I think of this? I'll fool them into thinking that I'm bringing water to the horse."

Moshichi had grown tired of the hard work of ladling ten buckets of water from the well every day. So, lying down in the room next to the stable, he made the sounds of the horse lapping up the water, while he heard Nizaemon's wife exclaim, "The horse is drinking a lot of water today. This must be because Moshichi works so hard."

"I did it!" Moshichi thought and, carried away with his success, continued on with his deception.

Even so, no one in the house suspected a thing, and Moshichi congratulated himself and laughed secretly in his heart.

After this, all that was left was to go out to the mountain and cut the hay, which he did perfunctorily; but he continued deceiving the others with the sounds of the horse lapping the water he couldn't be bothered to bring.

Neither Nizaemon nor the others in his household were aware of this.

"The horse certainly loves water," someone said.

"He's making great efforts to take care of it," said another.

But because Moshichi continued with his deception, the horse gradually weakened and lost weight. Nizaemon could not understand why. One night he peeked into the stable and was shocked. The horse had collapsed onto its side, was breathing heavily and seemed about to die.

"Moshichi! Moshichi!" he called out, and opened the door to the room where Moshichi was lying down.

"How strange! It drank so much water today," Moshichi lied. "And it always has plenty to drink. The poor thing. Maybe it's caught a disease that's been going around."

The horse died that night. All the members of Nizaemon's house cried and, with Moshichi's help, carried the horse to the mountain and buried it.

"Please erect a gravestone, no matter how small," Nizaemon said, and Moshichi did as he was bid.

◊　　◊　　◊

One day, some time later, when Moshichi was gathering firewood on the mountain, he heard the sound of a horse lapping water behind him and felt something wet dripping onto his back. Terrified, Moshichi ran in circles as if in a trance, but the sound of the horse lapping water would not go away. Suddenly, the sky went black and he collapsed exhausted. There, right before his eyes was the grave marker of the buried horse.

He then tried again to flee around and around through the forest, but at last fell straight down over a cliff into a valley stream and died.

Almost as though a witness to this, it seems that the sound of a horse lapping water continued for a long, long time.

A Moonflower the Color of Blood

War is a cruel and brutal thing.

The time was the Warring States period; the year, 1545. For Seki Morinaga, the proud and strong master of Wachino Castle in the Ina Valley, the day had come when his fortress finally fell. Unexpectedly attacked by his neighbor, Shomojo Tokiuji, whose power had increased, his castle was set aflame and he had ended his life within the castle grounds.

Well then, what about O-man, the wife he had left behind, and their son, the young Chogoro?

As the castle fell, O-man had already been resigned to her fate, and in the midst of the rising flames, she held her son and spoke to him with tears filling her eyes. "Chogoro, things having come to this pass, we can only go in the footsteps of your father."

But Chogoro, who was still a child nursing at his mother's breast, could not understand what she meant, and only cried and cried.

O-man had taken up a sword, but became confused at the pathos of her son's voice and her heart wavered.

"If we could escape . . . only for this child's sake . . ."

As the enemies were exulting over the castle going up in flames, O-man had escaped the burning building with her son. She sprang abruptly from a thicket and, watching the surroundings carefully, fled to the mountain to the rear of the castle. Heading toward the Wachino River, she quickly turned in the direction of the village where she had been born, and where she could imagine the faces of her mother and father who must have been so worried.

When she got to the Wachino River, however, she could see on the opposite bank the lights of a great number of torches. And these were probably not those of their allies. If they were discovered, their fate would be being burned at the stake or being beheaded. O-man turned around and fled frantically to the forest in the opposite direction.

On the evening of the third day, O-man stood totally exhausted and dazed in the forest, still holding the baby that no longer had the strength to even cry. Her body had been weakened by the continual summer rains, but just as she felt totally at a loss, she noticed a solitary farmer's hut built on a cliff in a clearing of the forest.

"That will do," she thought and, almost crawling, reached the eaves of the hut, prayerfully fed Chogoro from her breast and, mindful of her pursuers, begged the day to darken soon.

Just then, her eyes fell upon a moonflower displayed on a shelf in the farmer's hut. For a moment, her heart softened, she remembered the moonflowers at her house in her old hometown and fell into a trance. Of all the flowers, the white ones were the most beautiful . . . She remembered how her own mother had taken a single moonflower and had her hold it when she was young.

As her tears fell, she spontaneously reached out to the flower and put it into Chogoro's grasping little hand.

"Look. A flower."

With that, Chogoro's countenance, which had looked so pained, brightened up at once and he showed his mother a smile. O-man now embraced the belief that they would be able to stay alive and was resolved to continue their flight.

But suddenly, a silhouette appeared.

With an ugly gleam in his eye, a man looked up and down at O-man, who was wearing the tattered and torn remnants of what had once obviously been a stylish kimono.

"When did I say that I would give that flower to you?" he growled, lifting her chin in his hand and glowering at her face. "You damned thief!" he yelled and turned to his nearby hut and shouted, "Hey! A thief! This is a great catch!"

O-man immediately realized what that meant—the man had understood her social status.

Very soon, not only the people from the man's hut but

other villagers gathered noisily like excited insects and surrounded O-man and Chogoro. More than that, a number of
enemy samurai also appeared.

O-man looked around at the crowd of people and glared
back at them steadily. "You who would not allow me even a
single flower are human trash!" she said. "After I die together
with this child, all of your moonflowers will be the bright red
color of blood." And she thrust her way through the crowd
and leapt in an instant over the side of the cliff.

The following year, even though the moonflowers in the
garden of that farmer's hut bloomed fully, they were not a
beautiful white as before, but just as O-man had predicted,
were stained the bright red color of blood. On seeing this, the
farmer went insane, and after that, the house that had been
cursed never grew moonflowers again.

Or so it is said.

PART 14

HAIR-RAISING STORIES FROM THE NOT-SO-DISTANT PAST

The Man Who Could Drink
Two Quarts of Soy Sauce

Soy sauce is something you sprinkle on natto or dip raw fish into. But in this regard, there was a strange man indeed.

At a certain gathering . . .

"Soy sauce? What about it?" the man boasted. "I could easily drink two quarts of the stuff. As I'm a real man, I'll show you right now."

But the others said that if he drank that much, he'd come down with a fever and die on the spot.

"Well then, I'll show you," he laughed.

So the other people there brought in a two-quart bottle of soy sauce. Turning the bottle upside down, he put it to his mouth and gulped down all of it. And, as soon as he had drunk it all, he was showered with applause.

He then said, "All right, excuse me," and ran off in the direction of his house.

Everyone was impressed and declared the man to be "quite a fellow."

Nevertheless, there were some that wondered why the man returned home so quickly after drinking the soy sauce.

◊　◊　◊

Then one day in the village, the man was requested by some people around him to show them again.

"What do you mean?" the man said, pretending not to understand, and waiting for what might be said next.

"Soy sauce. Aren't you the one who drinks the soy sauce?"

The man laughed scornfully. "Well then," he said. "Let me show you."

Just as always, he lifted up the bottle filled with soy sauce that he carried and, full of his usual self-confidence, said that this would have no effect on his body at all. He then started to gulp the liquid down. Everyone thought that for sure he might die. They held their breath and watched him closely as he emptied the bottle.

His face immediately turned bright red. Someone asked if he was all right, and the man responded pridefully that, yes, indeed he was. Then came the applause, the man excused himself, and hurriedly left the room.

He then ran as fast as he could to his home and leapt into the bath in the garden. But then he screamed that he was done for. Very soon after, he was in agony and he could no longer breathe.

The truth of the matter was that on a day when it seemed he would be putting on his show of drinking soy sauce, he would secretly heat up the bath ahead of time and, as soon as he got home, soak in the bath and quickly sweat out the fever.

But someone had discovered his secret, gone to his house ahead of him and pulled the plug.

This was the wretched end of the man. But the man who pulled the plug to the bath hid his crime to the day he died, and his agony must have been great as well.

Sakata-san's Secret

It was sixteen years after the end of the Asian and Pacific War. Of those who had experienced the sorrow and pain of war, very few remained. But even now I cannot forget the story I heard of one man among those few. This is a secret about which I have not spoken of to his family even now, so provisionally, I am calling him Sakata-san.

One night, Sakata-san told me this story in a hushed voice.

"In the year 1945, before Japan's surrender in the September of that year, large cities like Tokyo were constantl being bombed in American air raids and turned into nothing but burnt fields. At that time, I was at the naval academy at Yokosuka and being instructed every day in military tactics by commissioned officers.

"One day, just as a single American airplane flew over the academy, there was something sounding like engine trouble high up in the air. At that moment, three red-haired American soldiers bailed out of the aircraft and parachuted into an open field. Those of us at the academy were immediately ordered by our officers to take them captive.

"They were prisoners of war, but we decided that we would kill them anyway."

Here, Sakata-san's voice suddenly became nothing more than a whisper. Under the orders of the officers, there was a secret plan. They were to lock up the American soldiers in the barracks until nighttime and then cut them down with swords at midnight. Even in times of war, killing enemy soldiers in cruel ways was prohibited by international law. Therefore, it was necessary to do this in secret.

Seven strong academy students were selected to carry out this cruel deed and Sakata-san was among them. Along with the officers, two instructors took them to the designated spot in a field near the academy, where they would later carry out the task.

"All right? Sharpen your swords well during the day," one of the officers said. "Cutting off a head is not as easy as you might think. It will take a good bit of strength." The officer then boastfully spoke of his own experience.

Sakata-san tried to calm his trembling, but thought of the face of the man whose head he was to cut off and the faces of his family. The men who had parachuted down were youths, not so different in age from him and his own companions.

As he tried to calm his vacillation, night came and a gibbous moon appeared in the sky. All the lights in the houses in the area of the silent field had been extinguished and the enemy soldiers were dragged out crying into the center of the field. Then they were made to dig with shovels the holes into which they would be buried after being beheaded. The holes had to be dug deep. And their digging had to be done in secret.

When the officer informed the three men that that was enough, he ordered Sakata-san and his companions to blindfold them and to tie their hands behind their backs. This having been done, the officer had them sit in front of the holes. He then had a large amount of sake passed around to Sakata-san and his men, and he himself got drunk too.

"All right, you men. Are you ready?" he grunted. "You will have to behead them one after another, so put all your strength into it. Are you resolved? You can't behead them all at once," and he demonstrated the cutting action, waving his own sword through the air.

As the moment approached, Sakata-san was filled with resolve, his heart beating furiously. But of the seven men, there was now the decision of which three men would be chosen to carry out the beheadings. Biting his lip, he prayed that it wouldn't be him.

"Sakata!" came the command. "We'll start with you." He was the very first.

Sakata's heart continued to beat furiously. No matter how

much sake he had put down, it was not enough to make him drunk. But when he tried to move, he couldn't.

"You!" the officer yelled. "The Japanese spirit! Don't you have the Japanese spirit?" and he struck him on the back.

This filled Sakata-san with the determination he needed and he answered, "Yes! I will follow your order!"

With this, he went up next to the quiet enemy soldier and drew his sword.

"Now! Do it!"

At this shouted command, he resigned himself, lifted his sword and struck at the enemy soldier's neck. But just as the officer had said, it was not so easily cut through, and in the end, the officer took his place and completed the act.

"I don't remember what happened to the other enemy soldiers, but it is certain that they met the same fate," Sakata-san recalled. "Still it was the first time I cut a man down with my own hands, and the last.

"Not long after that, we were defeated in the war and there was no reason to tell such stories to my family. Nowadays, Americans and Japanese mix together and laugh as though nothing had happened, but aren't there many people from my generation who had such experiences? We just don't talk about them. War, where human beings kill their own kind, should absolutely not be tolerated."

At the time Sakata-san told me this story, he ran a grocery store in a village in the mountains. He was an affable man and he was doing good business.

Who could think that this man had such a past?

The Woman inside the Hole in the Desk

You might think this strange and scary story is too crazy to be true, but it was told seriously by a very serious man called Kurita Shokichi.

This concerns the time when Shokichi had evacuated to Shinshu. As the Asia and Pacific War became more intense, more and more people living in the cities turned to their relatives or others in the countryside in order to flee the fires of war. Shokichi and his entire family came to Shinshu under such conditions.

The elementary schools at that time were called National Schools, and in the year of Japan's defeat in the war, he was in the fourth grade of such a school, commuting every day from his aunt's house.

On the morning of the first day attending this new school, after greeting the other students in the classroom, Shokichi was told by the young male teacher that his seat would be the farthest one down the aisle. It was a desk made of wood—unlike desks these days that are made of plastic. When he sat down, he thought that it was just right for him and he began to feel less anxious.

In Tokyo, Shokichi had run this way and that to escape the air raids and crept through the flames to survive, so just sitting peacefully like this must have been very pleasant for him. But from the very first day at his new school, he noticed that there was a strange hole about half an inch in diameter on the top of his desk. It was a rather old desk, with knife marks and ink stains here and there.

At first, Shokichi did not pay much attention to the hole, but one day when his studies were becoming difficult and the teacher had gone to the staff room for some reason or another, Shokichi chanced to peek with one eye into the hole.

"Huh?" He gave a little gasp.

He furtively looked around to see if anyone was watching, then once again focused his eye on the hole. Every time he peeked into it, his whole body shook.

"There . . . there's someone there . . ."

In the middle of the hole he could see the back of a crouching woman. Her long hair hung down to her shoulders and she was quiet and still. Around her was a vague light, giving the feeling of a small chamber in another world. But there was no way a person could have gotten inside such a small hole . . .

Wondering if this could be an illusion, Shokichi rubbed his eyes and then peeked in again. But it was not an illusion.

She was there. She was definitely there.

The woman crouched very still and she did not move at all. And he could sense that there was something sad about her back.

Shokichi could not sit still and felt like calling someone over, but thought he would be laughed at as a fool. He had just moved to the school, still had no friends and so lacked the courage to do anything. Thinking it through, he decided it would be his secret alone.

Looking stealthily down the hole, he whispered, "Hey."

With that, the woman looked up at him and Shokichi momentarily felt a fear that brought blood rushing to his face. The woman had neither eyes nor nose nor mouth. Shokichi trembled in fear and saw that tears were flowing from where her eyes might have been. Then, just as he felt that he could see her eyes, she beckoned to him as though appealing for something.

At that instant, the teacher called out "Hey! Kurita! Your face is completely pale."

Shokichi said he felt fine and, trembling, faced the teacher with a forced smile, then looked away.

"Ah, it's this desk," the teacher said coming up to him. "It's

terribly dirty, huh. And there's even a hole in it. I'll have you
sit somewhere else right now."

The teacher asked if he would like another desk from the
storeroom, but Shokichi replied that the one he had would
be fine, and quickly leaned over the desk. In his heart, he fervently wanted to solve the riddle of what he had just seen in
the hole.

The days passed. The smooth-faced woman began shedding tears of blood and continued beckoning to him, but he
could not understand what she wanted.

Yet, one day when the autumn wind was blowing, the eyes
that had not been there suddenly opened and the bloody
tears became a copious flow of bright red blood. Shokichi,
although he had become used to seeing the woman, was so
shocked, that in his haste to get away he fell off his chair. With
his heart racing, he went home to try to sleep, but his heart-
beat would not slow down.

When he returned to school on the Monday, the desk was
gone and he realized that the teacher could not remain indif-
ferent to what was going on and had replaced it.

Shokichi could not help but be disappointed and began
searching for the desk. Whenever he had a break, he continued to search, thrusting his way through the desks and chairs
stored in a small shed in the corner of the courtyard. But in
the end he was unable to find it.

◊   ◊   ◊

Seven years later, after Shokichi had graduated, he found out
that the storeroom shed had burned down. Which was to say
that the desk had also gone up in flames, he thought.

"Why in the world was that lady appealing to me?" he
wondered, and that question remained firmly inside of him
even when he became an adult.

In the end, after Shokichi witnessed so many people dying
in the air raids, he came to the conclusion that perhaps the
spirits of those who had died were filled with anger toward

the war, and had found such knotholes in which to secrete themselves.

This story, or perhaps Shokichi himself, may be seen as a hallucination from the fear caused by the tragedy of the air raids in Tokyo.

Whatever the truth of this story, the fact remains that Shokichi and the people of the world he lived in are no longer with us today.

The Bride's Regret

Traditionally in Japan, when women are married, they wear a *hana'yome* (lit. flower bride) outfit with a white headpiece that "hides their horns." According to many people nowadays, a dress would be fine as the bridal outfit, but long ago, a "dress" would have been unthinkable. This story takes place at such a time.

I was told this story by my close friend, Kenkichi, who had long whiskers, and whom we affectionately called Higesa—Mr. Whiskers. The story went as follows:

At one time, in any village or town, there was the custom of pounding mochi rice cake using a pestle and mortar at the end of the year, and that day came around in my town as well. Well, it was a very cold day, and when we had finished pounding the mochi in our house, I was asked by my father to take some pestles with my brother "up the slope," which was how we referred to my uncle's house. And so that is what we did. One of the pestles was large and heavy, while the other was small. I carried the small one, my older brother took the other, and we walked up the icy road, our feet making a crunching noise.

Behind our uncle's house at the top of the slope was a house where an old spinster lived. The woman was called Kei-chan, and the man to whom she was supposed to have had an arranged marriage had come down with lung disease and was rumored to be bedridden at home.

I once heard my grandmother say that Kei-chan was such a pretty and capable woman that she should have found a partner early in life. But now, she was a sad figure. And for sure, there were times when she stood in front of her house staring vacantly at the sky, her face almost transparently white and beautiful. In my child's heart, I was crushed by the story about how she never got married, and thought what a good wife she would have been.

Between my uncle's house and Kei-chan's, there was a bamboo thicket and there was a path through this thicket which came out at the entrance to my uncle's house. As my brother and I were taking this route, we could see that the door to Kei-chan's house, even on this cold day, was wide open and a light was coming from inside. We also saw an unfamiliar figure there, which was strange, and we hurried on toward the thicket.

At that moment, we uttered a cry!

A woman dressed in an old-fashioned hana'yome bridal gown appeared suddenly in the thicket, her eyes downcast in sorrow, then just as suddenly disappeared.

"What . . . what was that?" my brother asked. But my mouth was trembling and I could hardly speak. "You saw it, didn't you?"

We later found out that right at that moment, Kei-chan had died.

"Such a sad face. Surely, she had some regrets." Higesa said, and then fell silent.

He seemed to have never told this story to anyone, and this is understandable.

The Rolling-Tea-Bowl Ghost

This is a story told by an old lady living in a place called Habiro in the city of Ina.

A long time ago during the Taisho era at the beginning of the twentieth century, if you followed the road north from Habiro you eventually came to a small bridge. On the other side of the bridge was a slope, so heavily forested and dark you would feel uneasy walking there, even in the daytime. It was also rumored that the place was haunted by a "rolling-tea-bowl" ghost.

It is said that on a lonely night with neither stars nor moon, someone came along this slope, heard the sound of a rolling tea bowl—*garagara koron . . . garan koron*—shook with fear and fled to a nearby house.

It was feared that if you encountered this rolling tea bowl, you would be eaten up.

The old lady who told this story is no longer living, so we will never know if anyone ended up being killed and eaten by this ghost.

These days, in our crowded towns and cities where we live closely side by side, it's difficult to imagine that stories like this could be true. But if one night, you should find yourself on an icy and isolated mountain road, with the only sign of life the distant light of a solitary house, you may be more inclined to consider the truth of this old lady's tale.

The Woman Who Appeared Beyond the Shrine

A friend of mine told me about this scary experience he had as a child:

"This happened about the time I was eight or nine years old. At that time I lived in a village not so far away from Mount Kamuriki.

"One autumn evening, I was returning from the vegetable field, became separated from my father and took a different road home. The road led to a mountain mined for copper, was overhung on both sides with tree after tree, and gave one an uneasy feeling.

"The clouds of sunset were visible through the trees, but not enough to say whether it was a beautiful sunset or to predict what the weather might be tomorrow, and I could not settle into a calm frame of mind.

"Added to that, the sound of the rubber sandals I was wearing made me feel as though I was being followed and I got scared.

"When I hurried on with a quickened pace, I could see a small shrine dedicated to a fox on my left. And just then, I got a glimpse of something white beyond the shrine.

"I wondered for a moment if it was a rabbit, but when I looked carefully, it was a human being. It was, moreover, a woman in a white kimono, her hair was unkempt, and she had a very slender neck. Her neck quickly turned in my direction and the instant I saw her face, I thought it was a Kitsune fox demon.

"But it wasn't that at all, and she looked at me and laughed, her mouth split from one side of her face to the other, and her eyes upturned.

"I was shaking all over and ran down the slope as fast as I could. When I finally reached the mulberry field at the entrance to the village, which was on level ground, I was gasping for air, but I felt that I was safe.

"Even now, I can give no explanation for what that was."

My friend took a deep breath as he told this story to me, and I myself have had a similar experience. But as time has passed I think now that it must have been an illusion, and I never mention it to anyone.

Still, I cannot say if this story is true or not.

"Books to Span the East and West"

Tuttle Publishing was founded in 1832 in the small New England town of Rutland, Vermont [USA]. Our core values remain as strong today as they were then—to publish best-in-class books which bring people together one page at a time. In 1948, we established a publishing outpost in Japan—and Tuttle is now a leader in publishing English-language books about the arts, languages and cultures of Asia. The world has become a much smaller place today and Asia's economic and cultural influence has grown. Yet the need for meaningful dialogue and information about this diverse region has never been greater. Over the past seven decades, Tuttle has published thousands of books on subjects ranging from martial arts and paper crafts to language learning and literature—and our talented authors, illustrators, designers and photographers have won many prestigious awards. We welcome you to explore the wealth of information available on Asia at **www.tuttlepublishing.com**.

Published by Tuttle Publishing, an imprint of Periplus Editions (HK) Ltd.

www.tuttlepublishing.com

Shinshu Mukashi Gatari 1 Yokai Henge no Hanashi
Shinshu Mukashi Gatari 5 Fushigina Hanashi
© Noboru Wada, 2011, 2012
Illustrations © Haruna Wada 2011, 2012
English translation rights arranged with Shinanoki Shobo through Japan UNI Agency, Inc., Tokyo

English translation © 2023 William Scott Wilson

Library of Congress Catalog-in- Publication Data in progress

ISBN 978-4-8053-1758-7

26 25 24 23   5 4 3 2 1   2311VP
Printed in Malaysia

Distributed by:

North America, Latin America & Europe
Tuttle Publishing
364 Innovation Drive
North Clarendon
VT 05759 9436, USA
Tel: 1(802) 773 8930
Fax: 1(802) 773 6993
info@tuttlepublishing.com
www.tuttlepublishing.com

Asia Pacific
Berkeley Books Pte Ltd
3 Kallang Sector #04-01
Singapore 349278
Tel: (65) 6741-2178
Fax: (65) 6741-2179
inquiries@periplus.com.sg
www.tuttlepublishing.com

Japan
Tuttle Publishing
Yaekari Building, 3rd Floor
5-4-12 Osaki Shinagawa-ku
Tokyo 141 0032 Japan
Tel: 81 (3) 5437 0171
Fax: 81 (3) 5437 0755
sales@tuttle.co.jp
www.tuttle.co.jp